Games Girls Play

Also by Deanna Lee:

Undressing Mercy

Barenaked Jane

Exposing Casey

Published by Kensington Publishing Corporation

Games Girls Play

DEANNA LEE

𝒜

APHRODISIA

KENSINGTON BOOKS

http://www.kensingtonbooks.com

APHRODISIA BOOKS are published by

Kensington Publishing Corp.
119 West 40th Street
New York, NY 10018

ISBN-13: 978-0-7582-3499-5
ISBN-10: 0-7582-3499-6

First Kensington Trade Paperback Printing: July 2009

10 9 8 7 6 5 4 3 2 1

Printed in the United States of America

Contents

Dangerous Play

1

"Oh. My. God." I stared numbly at the television.

The phone started to ring as the reporter started to replay the video footage and I reached out for the phone. My hand connected with it and I dragged it to my ear. I swallowed hard as the replay of the video of my favorite client strutting out of a well-known BDSM club with not one but two women continued.

"Hello."

"Jesus H. Christ." Kristen Travis groaned in my ear. "Please say it's fake."

No. I knew the man well enough to know that it was him. Joshua Keller—every delicious inch of him encased in leather pants and a too-tight T-shirt—star soccer player, one of my mostly heavily endorsed clients, so James Bond British he practically gleamed in the sun, and much to my utter shock a sexual deviant.

I reached out and grabbed my DVR remote to record the footage. "Shit."

"Yeah." Kristen sighed. "Come on, Tara, what did we do to deserve this?"

"I don't know but my father was right. I should have gotten into corporate PR. It was a mistake specializing in athletes. Look at this crap!" I paused the recording when it centered on his face. "It's old."

"What?"

"Unless he's shaved off his goatee this is old; at least six months."

Six months old. Yes, at least six months and we could manage that. Couldn't we? My company was entirely too new for me to fail at handling such a public display of bad judgment on the part of one of my biggest clients. Sure, Joshua had never been a choirboy and when he'd come to Atlanta he'd brought with him a reputation for loud parties, indiscreet women, and barhopping.

"Yeah. You're right. He's very attached to the facial hair. I tried for three hours to get him to shave last week for that modeling gig. He outright refused."

I was glad; the look was dead sexy, and if I were right, it would certainly help defuse the situation that was quickly developing. "Has this hit national news yet?"

"No, but it's on the web so it's just a matter of time before we start getting phone calls asking for statements. Even if it's old, it's still brand-*new* news."

She was right and that presented a problem that I did not want to think about. Though getting one of my clients on a national news broadcast had appeal, one normally hoped for charity events, not innuendos of threesome sex and BDSM clubs.

"Did you have any idea he had . . . ?" Kristen paused. "How exactly can we spin it? I mean if he likes to tie up women and spank them . . ."

I pursed my lips and glared at the television; the mere thought of him enjoying something like that had my pulse racing in a very different way. As sexy as the man was I'd never seriously considered hooking up with him because I'd figured he wouldn't be up for that kind of rough sex play.

"Men won't care, but women . . . At least some will try to paint him as a misogynist who gets off on hitting women."

"Yeah, that's *so* not good." Kristen groaned.

I jumped at the sound of my doorbell and stood from the couch. "I have to go. Someone's at the door."

"I'll try to figure out what to say besides 'no comment.'"

"Yeah." Though I wasn't all that convinced there was a damn thing anyone could say that would make the situation any better.

I went to the front door of my apartment, still clutching the phone, and jerked it open. Joshua. The man looked like sin, the kind of sin my mama had assured me would send me straight to hell. A year and a half of being his publicist and I still couldn't look at him without my panties getting wet.

I glanced over his face, taking in the still-present goatee, his short black hair, his finely chiseled face, and nice very kissable mouth before I met his gaze with my own. Dark blue eyes stared back at me, intense and thoughtful. He'd been at my home once in all the time that I'd known him and that had been for a company dinner party.

"You know I prefer to meet clients in my office."

"I didn't figure this could wait until tomorrow."

I stepped back and motioned him inside. "Already getting questions?"

"Phone and e-mail." He shoved his hands into his pockets as he stopped in front of my television. "HD?"

"Of course." I sat down on the couch and watched him as he started to pace. The black slacks he wore molded quite nicely to his ass with each turn.

Objectifying men was something of a hobby, and my job was totally to blame. I spent all day selling some of the finest bodies on the planet for advertising and endorsement. It was a bit disturbing how much of a product I viewed some of them. "How old is it and do you have any idea who recorded it?"

"At least a year. I haven't been in the Playground in a long time and I have no idea who filmed it or what else they might be sitting on. I haven't always been discreet about my sexual liaisons but I've put a serious effort into behaving since . . . well, for a while now." He stopped pacing and turned to face me. His expression spoke volumes about the state of his temper. The barely leashed anger was oddly attractive.

"Okay." I took a breath and tried to refocus. "At least that's something. We can say that video is old and try to leave it at that."

"Don't yank me around, Tara." He motioned toward the television. "We live in the freaking south and the people around here are so repressed that I'll be some hell-bound pervert inside the next twelve hours."

"At least we won't have to worry about the metrosexual factor anymore."

He stilled completely and turned to glare at me. "Pardon me?"

"We've had feedback that perhaps you were too fashionable, too put together to be straight." I pursed my lips. "It's not really a problem among your female fans and now that male fans think you've lived out their favorite sexual fantasy . . . They were twins, right?"

He looked briefly at the television before focusing on me entirely. "Yes, I believe so. So what kind of fallout am I looking at?"

"I doubt you'll lose any of your endorsement deals; we might have to do an interview or two. You'll have to discuss and if necessary downplay your role in the lifestyle. You're a Dom, right?"

He raised one eyebrow but gave a short nod. "But I'm not a sadist."

"No, you didn't strike me as that type."

But suddenly Joshua did seem to be the sort of man who might like to control every aspect of a sexual encounter. How on earth had I missed it? I crossed my legs and tried to get comfortable on the couch. I really missed sitting behind my desk in a suit; at home in shorts and a T-shirt I didn't feel nearly as powerful and in control as I figured I needed to be to deal with a man like him.

"You bloody Americans . . ." He paused and flushed. "Sorry."

"We're not all sexually repressed religious zealots." I bit down on my lip, stunned that I had let the words fall out of my mouth. "I mean, not everyone is going to think you're going to hell."

He was silent as he crossed the distance that separated us and took a seat on the couch beside me. "What do you think?"

"Why does it matter what I think?" I took a deep breath as he picked up one of my hands and held it between his. "Joshua?"

"You're going to be making statements and answering questions about this for the next few weeks. At least until some starlet is photographed without panties. I need to know if knowing this about me disgusts you or makes you feel differently about me. If it does . . ." He rubbed his thumb across the top of my hand. "I need to know you're in my corner on this, Tara. That's why I'm here. I could give a fuck what most people think. I'd land on my feet professional if things went to shit here in Atlanta. What I need to know is that I've got you on my side."

My fingers tightened against his even as I relaxed beside him. "Did you know that you're the only single client I have who has never once hit on me?"

Deanna Lee

He laughed softly, brought my hand up to his mouth, and kissed it gently. "You deserve better than a man like me."

"Is that so?" The thought was a little irritating. I deserved a lot and I figured a man like him could do a lot to set my world to rights. My body was already humming at the possibilities.

"I travel too much and let's not forget"—he jerked his head toward the television—"I'm a bit pervy."

Hadn't I thought the same thing just minutes earlier? Of course, truth be known I was just as deviant as he was. I liked a little pain and a lot of dominance with my sex. I'd never gone to a club like the Playground, not because I wouldn't have enjoyed myself but because I was afraid that I would enjoy it too much.

The last man I had dated had been so vanilla that I'd practically fallen asleep during sex one night. I'd ended it before I wound up embarrassing myself.

Joshua's thumb brushed over the top of my hand where his lips had been all too briefly and I straightened up.

"Well, we have plans to make."

His grip tightened as I started to leave the couch. "Tara."

What could I say that wouldn't reveal my true position on his lifestyle choices? I forced myself to relax back against the couch. "I'm not disturbed by discovering you like . . ." What the hell did he like? He'd said he wasn't a sadist but had offered little other explanation. "Please tell me you're the average run-of-the-mill guy with control issues and an occasional need to spank a woman's ass."

I turned to look at his face just as his mouth dropped open. "Excuse me?"

"Look, reporters are going to find those two women and they are going to be interviewed and they are going to talk about all the freaky sex you did have and probably make some

8

stuff up, too. Do you get off on any extreme fetish play and if you do, did you with those two women?"

"Most would consider any aspect of BDSM extreme fetish play," he replied softly, obviously unwilling to answer the question.

"Yeah, well, I'm not most people." *Fuck*. That was not what I meant to say.

"Are you asking me for a play-by-play description of my sexual exploits with two women from over a year ago? I don't even remember their names!"

I jerked my fingers free from his hand and bolted up off the couch. "Well, we'd damn well better find out their full names so you'll know who they are. Otherwise, you'll be a hell-bound man-whore deviant who's slept with so many women he's forgotten half of them."

"Man-whore?" he asked, his voice low with shock.

"Well, you did take home two strange women." I took a step back as he stood. "That's certainly man-whorish behavior. And what's up with the leather pants?"

He glanced toward the TV and crossed his arms over his chest. "They suited the occasion. As for your question, no— I'm not into anything extreme. At the most, I probably tied those two women up, spanked them a little, and made them beg for my cock. Which I'm sure I gave to both of them repeatedly until I could not move. But honestly, I don't remember the night specifically; they aren't the last pair of women I've had in my bed."

Beg for his cock. My mouth watered, my nipples tightened against the soft material of my T-shirt, and wetness rushed between my labia at that naughty thought. I cleared my throat and tried to push back the unexpected slap of lust that rushed over my body. "Is that your kick, then? Two women?"

"No, not normally." His gaze roamed over me, lingered on my breasts, and then focused on my face. "Frankly, very little has satisfied me over the last year and a little excess goes a long way toward making a man forget that."

"Well, stop that! No more double dipping until this blows over." I pointed my finger at him and took another step back when he glared at me. "It's my job to manage your public image."

"It's not your job to tell me who I can stick my dick into."

I flushed and my gaze immediately dropped to his crotch. "Well, you and your penis have made enough of a mess already so for the next good while I *am* going to be telling you where you can and cannot stick it!"

"Then I suggest you stop talking to it because despite what you women might think that head doesn't make the decisions."

I jerked my gaze back up to his face, stunned that I'd actually been staring at his groin, and blushed. "I wasn't talking to your dick, you jerk."

"Could have fooled me."

My phone started to ring and I made an immediate grab for it. Talking to anyone would be better than continuing this conversation. "Hello."

"It's on CNN."

Sonya Carson. She was the third member of my PR firm and another close friend. Both she and Kristen worked their butts off with me to get the Marcus Group off the ground. They were like sisters; only I never had to worry about them tattling to my daddy when I did something they didn't like. I glared at Joshua as I perched on a chair a few feet from the couch.

"Great."

"Our answering service is losing their mind," Sonya chuckled. "God, he looks hot in those pants. Of course, honestly, he looks hot in just about anything. I bet you five bucks those two women are already arranging to get paid for a tabloid interview."

"No doubt."

"I told you taking him on would be difficult."

She had. Repeatedly. I glanced toward him and found him pacing in front of the still-paused television. "Yeah, I remember."

"Have you had any contact with him?"

"He's standing in front of my new flat-panel television plotting something. He's either going to steal the TV or try to reach through it to strangle himself." Joshua flashed me a grin and walked back to the couch. "The video is at least a year old, so someone has sat on this for a while. Maybe they didn't realize it was him and only just discovered they'd caught someone famous on their camera."

"Or they have more goodies to share and that's just the start. I think we'll see another video or maybe pictures any day now."

"Well, it isn't like the world hasn't seen his bare ass already." I glared at him when he laughed. It was one of the reasons my company had been hired to manage his image. He'd been caught in the Bahamas skinny-dipping with a woman. "And a sex tape could make us all some money."

"That's un-fucking-believable. . . ." He stopped, obviously at a loss as to how to deal with such a prospect.

"Kristen is running through ideas for a public statement and we still need to get in touch with Joshua's agent. In the meantime, tell the answering service that they can stop taking phone calls for our firm and please do not turn our voicemail on. I don't want five hundred messages waiting for us tomorrow."

He was back up and pacing by the time I hung up the phone. "Gary is on vacation with his wife and kids. I'm sure he'll call me as soon as he gets back to his hotel room and catches wind of this."

Gary Moorsey was his agent and had been since the day Joshua had come to the United States. "Don't you think we should call him?"

"He told me he wasn't carrying his cell phone to freaking Disney World. I'm sure he's trying to play grab-ass with Snow White even as we speak."

I couldn't help but laugh. Gary was from all accounts faithful to his wife but he was fond of the female ass in such a way that I always made sure that he never got in proximity of mine.

How bad was it really? Atlanta's new soccer star coming out of a fetish club with two women? I bit down on my bottom lip. It was bad enough. It would amuse men, outrage militant feminists, and set the devoutly religious on a tirade that could last for months.

"So what else are you hiding?"

"Pardon me?"

"Look, I was under the impression that you were keeping your nose clean. No skinny-dipping, no loud parties with barely clothed college girls, and the last time I checked you were dating a very respectable lawyer. Now look at you." I waved my hand toward the television.

"That *is* a year old, at least," he reminded me through clenched teeth. "I have done my level best to remain within the image plan you set up for me. I don't drink to excess, not even at home. I wear the right clothes, with the right logos. I wear the right fucking shoes when I run on my own goddamned street. I joined the gym you suggested; I go to the parties you determine are good for my image."

Okay, so he was mad. I forced myself to remain perfectly still under his gaze as I considered what I should say. I knew he hated the endorsement deals, the image management. It wasn't hard to imagine how it must have felt to wear workout clothes not because they were comfortable but because someone paid him to. "Okay, so the lawyer?"

"She started hinting that she wanted a ring. So I pushed her off."

He said it as if she'd demanded he get a sex change or something. "Joshua." His name left my mouth in an exasperated rush.

"What?" he demanded. "Can't a man find a steady piece of ass who won't be mentally shopping for a wedding dress within six months?"

"You're twenty-nine years old."

"So?"

"Don't you want to have some sort of permanent relationship?"

"Not with a workaholic lawyer who put my bank balance at the top of the 'yes' column of her list of reasons to marry me."

I tried not to laugh. Honestly. But he looked so genuinely . . . vexed that I couldn't help it. I laughed, hard. When I could I brushed away tears, took a deep breath, and asked the question that got me into so much delicious trouble. "Was 'he spanks my ass' at the top of her 'no' column?"

His lips tightened into a thin line and he stilled. "Are you baiting me on purpose or are you genuinely interested in what it would feel like to have the flat of my hand on that pretty ass of yours?"

I clamped my mouth shut to keep it from dropping open in shock and cleared my throat. "I think we should continue this discussion in my office in the morning." Standing up from the chair, I begged myself not to blush and walked toward my front door. It was mission essential that I get him out of my apartment as fast as possible.

He caught my arm as I passed him and pulled me toward him with a quick jerk. I sucked in a deep breath as he brought me around to face him. "You didn't answer my question, love."

"Don't call me that." I looked over his pretty face and tried to remind myself that I was in front of one of the biggest womanizers I knew. "And don't look at me like you want me, either."

Joshua used his free hand to touch my face, trailing his fingers along the line of my jaw. My stomach clenched as I imagined those same gentle fingers moving down my throat to the swell of my breast. Would they be firm, knowing on my nipples, or tentative? Would he explore a woman or take her over in a rush of physical pleasure? The thought of either option had my pulse racing and my mind reeling.

The consequences of getting involved with a client, especially one like him, were overwhelming. It wasn't easy running a PR firm in a male-dominated world where millions of dollars were tossed around like confetti. I hadn't gotten to where I was without ambition and self-control. For a year, I'd managed to keep my small attraction to him a secret, yet now all of that was falling to pieces around me.

"Why shouldn't I want you?"

"You said that I deserve better than a man like you." I lifted my chin and tried to look unaffected.

"Yes." He pulled me close and brushed his lips over mine. "I certainly did. I'm too hard for a woman like you. I play too rough. It would be dangerous for us to indulge in such desires."

I bit back a moan as he kissed his lips across my jaw and then downward along the column of my throat. "Joshua."

"Are you just curious, love?" He released my arm and slid both hands down my back and over my ass. "Or are you excited because you *know* what kind of pleasure we can give each other?"

Each brush of his lips, the soft sweeping motions of his hands, belied the hard and unyielding lover I assumed he would be. "This can't happen."

Why the hell wasn't I pushing him away? My body relaxed in his hold, accepted the way his hands maneuvered and controlled me. Control. I craved it on some deep level I could barely fathom. Perhaps I always had. Everything about my professional world was within my control. The desperate need to grab a hold of my life and my future had driven me through college at a breakneck pace, forcing me into the business world with a small loan and a fierce need to survive and succeed.

Yet I also knew that sacrificing control could be just as rewarding. That power in the hands of the right person could drive me to the brink of madness, give me pleasure so intense that remembering it could make me come.

He slid one hand over my hip and upward across my rib cage, and captured one aching breast before I could figure out his intentions. His thumb brushed over my nipple. It hardened even further and I locked my knees together to keep from leaning fully into his embrace. "It can happen if you let it."

Could I? It went against every rule I had. The thought of giving myself over to this man had me weak with anticipation. Would our professional relationship survive such a shift in our personal dynamics? "We shouldn't."

He pinched my nipple and a bolt of pleasure/pain shot right to my pussy. My body dampened, soaking the crotch of my panties instantly.

"Do you want to know what turns me on, Tara? Do you want to know what sort of deviant things really get me off?" His teeth sank into my earlobe between each question. "Then tomorrow, you can sit in your office, your pussy empty and aching for my cock while you answer questions about me and tell the world what an average, everyday kind of guy I am."

A shudder ran down my back as he pressed closer. His cock rubbed against my belly and the bottom of my world fell out.

15

No, there was *nothing* average about him. He moved me backward until my back met with the wall.

"Say yes." His mouth brushed over my pulse point, the silky hair of his goatee providing just enough stimulus to make my eyes cross. "Let me have you."

It was such a mistake. Such risks were the playgrounds of other women . . . women who didn't pin their dreams and their future on their ability to control the world around them.

"My safe word is *water lily.*"

2

Joshua lifted away from me abruptly and our eyes met. Carefully he planted both hands on either side of my head and studied me. After a few moments of utter silence he took a deep breath. "And what sort of pleasure and pain do you enjoy, love?"

"I'm a sexual submissive; not a slave or a pet." I bit down on my lip and closed my eyes; just saying the words relaxed something deep inside me. "It's been a long time since I've admitted that to anyone."

"You can trust me."

Yes. I knew that I could. "I enjoy pain to a degree. I'm not into humiliation, but bondage can be stimulating."

"And me without my toys." He used the tip of his finger to stroke my collarbone. "How long has it been since you've had a lover who catered to *all* of your needs?"

It had been years but was I prepared to admit that? I cleared my throat. "I was dating a man earlier in the year."

"That's not what I asked." Joshua chuckled when I looked away. "Strip."

I hesitated and bit down on my bottom lip. "I don't think . . ."

"Ready to use your safe word already? Come now, love, I thought you were up for this kind of play." He leaned in close to me, his mouth grazing mine in a gentle brushing of lips.

Joshua Keller was dangerous and so out of my league. I'd fantasized about the man a few times, but the sex had never been the kind he was offering me now. Honestly, my fantasy life could have been a lot more interesting if I'd known he had a freaky side.

"Strip."

His tone left no room for discussion or protest unless I wanted to use my safe word to back out of the situation. I was honest enough with myself to know that I wasn't going to deny myself the pleasure of him. Even if tomorrow I regretted it, at least I would have something hot and dirty to regret.

I jerked my T-shirt over my head and tossed it aside. His eyes dropped from my face to my breasts as he stepped back from me and gave me room to continue. I jerked off my socks, shorts, and panties and stood before him naked. My nipples tightened further at the exposure and the attention. I knew I had a good body; I took care of myself. Working with professional athletes could be hell on a woman's self-esteem and earning their respect took a lot of work. Being physically and mentally fit put me on top of my game and theirs.

He cleared his throat. "Bedroom?"

"You look nervous." I lifted one eyebrow. "My body isn't what you expected?"

"Christ, woman, you know you look like a walking wet dream." Joshua pulled me abruptly forward and rested his forehead on mine as his hands slid down my bare back. "I value your presence in my life, Tara. I don't want to ruin it. I spent the last year drowning myself in women to avoid making a move on you."

"Usually by the time I get naked for a man we're past this indecision thing."

"Yeah." One hand slid over my rib cage and upward to cup my breast. His thumb brushed over the nipple and I shuddered in his arms. "Promise me you won't push me out of your life."

It was a hefty promise to make and I swallowed hard as I considered it. I never gave my word lightly. Could I handle having him around when he got tired of me? "Let's promise not to lie or mislead each other."

"Done."

His mouth sank into mine, his tongue thrusting between my lips with skill and care. Hands that had been gentle, exploring, went firm and demanding as he pushed me back against the wall. The change was stunning: gone was the soft, seductive man that had maneuvered me out of my clothes and in his place was a hard, clearly dominant man that had my body nearly vibrating at the possibilities.

Joshua lifted his head; his eyes were darker and intent on my face. "Let's go play, love."

I slipped onto the bed and assumed the position he'd ordered shortly after I showed him my toy drawer. Never one to collect a wide variety of toys or equipment, I had a few vibrators, a leather flogger, and several lengths of cotton rope.

"We'll have to expand on your collection, love."

I kept my face pressed against the pillow, my eyelids tightly shut as he trailed the leather tresses of the flogger down the middle of my back and over my ass.

"You are a beautiful puzzle, woman." The bed dipped under his weight and I sucked in a breath when he slid astride my thighs. His cock rubbed briefly between the cheeks of my ass before sliding right between my legs. "So strong and confident yet obviously aching to be dominated. I am honored that you've put your pleasure in my hands."

He moved forward and the head of his cock bumped my

clit. A shudder ran the length of my back and I fought the urge to thrust back against him. "Oh, God."

"No, don't move." He ran his hands over my arms. "I normally have a much more formal discussion with a potential partner before we get to this stage." He brushed my hair over away from my neck and placed a soft kiss there. "Yet the mystery of you is exciting. Your little collection of toys offers a few tantalizing glimpses into your private world."

He lifted up and his hand fell abruptly and hard on my ass. I hissed at the sharp sting of it and lifted my hips up off the bed in a demand for more. A mistake, I knew, but I figured he might let me get away with it. I was wrong. He pushed me back onto the bed with one hand on the small of my back and delivered another blow. The smack of his skin against mine and the heat spreading from my ass to the rest of my body had me straining against his hold with no regard to the sort of punishment he might dish out.

Suddenly he was gone, and I groaned at the loss of physical contact.

"On your knees, face the headboard." I complied and swallowed hard when he wrapped a piece of rope around my wrists, binding them together tightly. Then he secured me to the wrought-iron headboard of my own bed. "Do not move. Do not come until you're told. Your body belongs to me. Do you understand?"

"Yes, sir."

Joshua slid up behind me and pressed his cock, hard and wet at the tip, against my ass. One hand snaked around and pressed against my stomach to pull me flush against him. "A year is little time to forget such basic things as obedience. Do you have any formal training?"

I could have lied and said no, but I'd already promised him honesty. "Yes, years ago in college. My roommate was Dom. She introduced me to the lifestyle."

He cupped my breasts with both hands and twisted my nipples between his fingers. "Did she fuck you?"

"No, but she could make me come." I let my head fall back against his shoulder and bit back a moan as he tightened his grip on my nipples. Pain shot from the tips of my breasts and slid right into my pussy with all the finesse of a fist. It was delicious and I wanted more, desperately.

"So naughty, love. Is she the only woman who has ever topped you?"

"Yes." I closed my eyes, my body tight with anticipation. "She liked the cane."

"And did you?"

"In her hands, yes. I've never let anyone else use one . . ."

"I understand," Joshua murmured. "Perhaps one day you'll trust me enough."

His lips brushed my shoulder and then he nipped my skin with his teeth. I loved the sharp pleasure of a well-placed bite, and when he did it again I arched in his arms despite myself. With a sigh he lifted his head and his fingers tightened on my nipples briefly before releasing them. Blood rushed back into my distended flesh immediately and I hissed between clenched teeth as the pleasure of it slowly ebbed away leaving me twisted with the want for more.

He moved away from me and I hung my head, my body tensed with anticipation. "You want this too much for it to be a punishment."

I almost laughed because he was so right.

Joshua snapped the flogger in the air above my back and I sagged against the headboard in disappointment. He chuckled softly. "I should deny you the bite of your favorite toy. I should bury my cock in that pretty pussy of yours and ride you like a whore until you have no choice but to come. Then leave you aching for this. . . ."

I gasped and jerked against the rope that bound me at the first stinging lash. Pleasure and pain ripped through my body like lightning, leaving no cell untouched. The effects of the blow started to fade just as he struck again. It ebbed and flowed over me in an endless wave of hot sticky pain that turned to pleasure in a heart-pounding instant. I pressed my thighs together in an effort to relieve the dull throbbing that rippled over my clit.

"Spread your legs."

With a moan, I did as he ordered. Cool air rushed over the exposed flesh of my cunt and I closed my eyes. It had been years since a man had turned me on so much and he'd barely touched me. Softly spoken words, the mere promise of punishment and a pounding cock had reduced me to a state of near-begging.

"You lack discipline." He smacked my ass in reprimand and I pursed my lips in what I could only describe as a pout, heaven help me. "If we are to play this game properly, love, you'll have to do much better. Else I'll be forced to *take* what I want and punish you in the only way I can: by ignoring your needs."

I shuddered at the thought, realizing that he probably would do just that. The blame would rest solely with me and my inability to obey. I'd started this game and made it clear that I wanted this from him, but I was, in my selfishness, ignoring his needs.

"I'll be good."

"Is that so?" He flicked the flogger lightly over my lower back and I swallowed the disappointment.

"Yes, sir."

The thin, flat leather tresses of the flogger drifted across my ass, down my thighs, and over my legs, only to travel back up in an agonizing path of the softest kind of stimulation.

"You lied to me."

"No, sir." I shook my head in denial.

He laughed. "You said that you enjoyed pain to a *degree,* but let's be honest, love, you're a pure-to-the-bone masochist. Your body is primed, ready to be used."

I started to deny it but he cut off my words by pushing two fingers into my cunt. My juices coated his fingers instantly and I clamped down on the invasion involuntarily. "Joshua." His name burst from my mouth more like a prayer than anything else and I swallowed hard to keep from saying more.

He leaned down and nipped my shoulder. "How much would it take to make you come, love? Have you always responded so well to pain?"

I couldn't answer; the words clogged in my throat as he pulled his fingers free and used the flogger to strike my thighs. The leather slapped around my legs, stinging and biting into my flesh with precision. His skill and care became evident then, as each blow landed differently and never in the exact same place—the perfect amount of stimulation. Never hard enough to bruise or break skin. It had been years since I'd been in the hands of someone so gifted. The difference was training. He was not like the straightlaced men I'd talked into spanking my ass over the years. Joshua was the real deal, and if I were going to be technical the first male Dom to ever get me in such a position. Could he tell?

My heart thudded hard and fast against my rib cage, my clit matching it beat for beat. I pushed off the need to come, determined that I would wait until he was ready. My fingers ached against the hold I had on the iron railing in front of me, and I hated myself for the months that I'd denied myself this. Surely, if I'd acted on my initial attraction, we could have worked our way into exploring our fetishes quickly enough. I'd never been shy about asking sex partners for something a little more than the straight edge . . . even if I rarely got it.

23

I lowered my head between my arms and closed my eyes as the pressure and the need built. Pain and pleasure snaked inside me, pulling at my insides and making me feel empty. I was ready for so much more, and, as if he knew it, he suddenly stopped and dropped the flogger beside me on the bed.

I looked to my left and watched out of the corner of my eye as he left the bed and found a condom in my toy drawer. He brought the box he'd just opened with him and dropped it near the flogger. I wet my lips as I watched him roll the condom onto his long, thick cock and wondered briefly if at some point during the evening he would let me suck him.

He came back to the bed, slid up behind me, and ran his hands down my back. I cried out, my overstimulated flesh immediately warming and responding to his touch. I arched against him and closed my eyes as he gripped my hips and pushed his cock into me with one harsh, deep stroke. The sharp sting of penetration brought another strangled cry from my lips.

Joshua's fingers curled into my hips, his short nails scoring my skin as he started to move. He withdrew and plunged deep with measured strokes over and over again as I clung to the headboard. My orgasm twisted and turned under my skin with each push of his cock. I wanted him to use me, to ride me like a whore as he'd suggested earlier, so I ignored the need to come and focused on him as he worked his cock in and out of my pussy. My muscles clenched on each inward thrust in an effort to keep him inside me and the soft gasping groans that slipped from his mouth told me he enjoyed it.

His hands drifted up my back, one stopping to grip my shoulder and the other moving into my hair. He fisted his hand into my hair as he increased his pace.

"Come for me, Tara. Come now."

Relief and disappointment warred inside me. I wasn't ready for this to end but my body was nearly begging me for relief. I forced myself to relax and when I let go my pussy rushed wet around him and I came hard, screaming his name.

He jerked me back hard against him, his pelvic bones flush against my ass as he came. After a long moment, he loosened his hold on me and as he pulled his cock from my body I clenched down on him in one final effort to keep him with me. He smacked my ass with a soft laugh and left the bed.

Several minutes passed before Joshua returned to the bed. He massaged my wrists as he pulled the rope free and tossed it aside. Then he carefully maneuvered me onto my side and pressed me close against his chest as he rested on the bed with me. Both of our bodies were damp with sweat, and when I let my hand rest on his chest I felt a near echo of my own heartbeat.

He pressed a soft kiss to my forehead and closed his eyes briefly. "If you regret this tomorrow I'm turning you over my knee and spanking you."

I chuckled. "Not much of a threat."

"No. Not much at all." He combed his fingers through my hair and sighed. "So, are you a natural redhead or not?"

Lifting my head, I raised an eyebrow. "Huh?"

"On most women I'd know by now but I never expected you to be the type to wax it all off."

"Oh." I frowned when I felt my cheeks heating. "You don't like it?"

"I plan to spend several hours showing you exactly how much I like it, after I rest a bit." He lifted my chin and placed a soft kiss on my lips.

"Yes, I'm a natural redhead. Though I have some highlights that I pay a pretty little penny for." I rolled onto my back and rubbed the damp flesh of my stomach. "You are a superior fuck."

"Yes. I know." He laughed softly and met my gaze. "As are you."

I couldn't help but grin. "Yeah."

Joshua leaned down and sucked one of my softening nipples into his mouth. Gently, as if I might break, he ran his tongue over it repeatedly, making the flesh rigid once more. He released it with a light pop and leaned back to study his handiwork.

"This woman from college . . ."

"She taught me the pleasure of giving up control." I bit down on my lip. I rarely if ever discussed Elise, but I had already admitted to my past. "She was older than me—close to thirty but back in school to get her degree in business. We shared an off-campus apartment. Elise was . . . open to relationships with both men and women. I thought I was curious about lesbian sex."

"But you weren't?"

"No. I'd accidently walked in on her with a woman. She had her tied up and was working her over like a hostage . . . to her obvious enjoyment. I stood there and watched, unable to move, and within a few minutes Elise made her come just by hitting her with a riding crop."

I closed my eyes briefly. The image of that young woman was seared into my brain. She'd sagged against the ropes that she was bound with and had sobbed nearly uncontrollably. I'd never had an orgasm like that in my life at the time. "I forced myself to leave and I thought Elise hadn't seen me."

"You were wrong."

"Oh, yes." I laughed softly. "I started to avoid her, but mostly because I kept imagining her fucking me. I couldn't get it out of my head and it didn't make any sense at all. I'd never been interested in sex with a woman. Eventually she cornered me and demanded that I explain myself. I tried to explain, tried to apologize for spying on her and her lover. Then finally I admitted that I kept thinking about it and that I thought that I wanted to have sex with her."

"She corrected you."

"Oh, yes." I blushed. The lesson was still fresh in my mind even seven years later. "She told me that I was a silly girl and that of course I wasn't a lesbian. I was as far from lesbian as a woman could get. It was the pain I wanted, the loss of control I craved. She offered it to me. Offered to show me what I really wanted."

"And you agreed?"

"Not for weeks. I was mortified. I couldn't fathom how I could possibly want someone to tie me up and hit me with a whip. It seemed abnormal and so very wrong." I relaxed against him and sighed when his fingers started to drift in a lazy pattern over my stomach. "I was so fucked up about it that I almost moved out. I was also pretty convinced that she was wrong and that I probably was a lesbian."

He laughed. "So stubborn."

"Yes. So, I decided that I would just experiment. I took my ass to a bar where I knew I could pick up a woman . . . found a soft, very feminine-looking woman who had warm eyes and a nice smile. I went home with her."

"Christ."

I glanced from his rapidly hardening cock to his face. "Men are so easy."

Joshua laughed. "Yeah, we are. But just think how messed up relationships would be if we weren't?"

"Yeah, there is that. Anyway, I went home with her but it became very evident that I was *not* a lesbian. We laughed, had drinks, ate a meal together, and then she sent me home." I smiled. "It was very nice kissing her, though. She had a soft mouth and tasted really good."

He slid astride my body with astounding speed. "You'll be the death of me."

"Yeah, but life is about the living not the dying." I rubbed his thighs and shifted under him as he rubbed the head of his cock against my stomach.

"Tell me the rest."

"One night, I couldn't stand it anymore. I had to know. So I banged on her door . . . and demanded her help."

"Demanded?"

"Oh, yes." I laughed softly. "I paid a harsh price for that little bit of attitude. She jerked me into her room, shoved me onto the bed with my ass in the air, pulled up my little night-gown, and spanked me until I cried. I came twice."

"And you had your answers." He ran his hands roughly over my breasts and caught my nipples in a vicelike grip.

"Yes. After she punished me, she held me and told me everything she thought I needed to know about the experience I had and perhaps the experiences that I might enjoy. Then she offered to train me. We made an agreement, determined my hard limits, and got started." I sucked in a breath as he twisted and pulled at my nipples. "Through experiment and a year of sessions I learned what I needed, preferred, and that it was all right to want those things."

I watched his face, waiting for some expression that would tell me what he thought of my story. I'd only revealed the depth of my experience to one other man, a man so far from the BDSM lifestyle that he might as well had been a puritan. He'd called me a dyke and a whore as he practically ran from my apartment. That had been more than four years ago and at most the men after him got the heavy-handed hint that I might like a little slap on the ass as they fucked me. Most of them had obliged but never at the level I needed or wanted.

"You were lucky. In the wrong hands you could have suffered. This woman did you a tremendous service and I hope you were properly grateful." He released my nipples as I relaxed beneath him. The delightful sting lingered as blood rushed back into the offended flesh. Joshua slid upward, his thighs pressing up against my breasts as he leaned forward and rubbed the head of his cock between them. "Suck me."

Wetting my lips, I wrapped one hand around him as he moved upward to rub against my lips. I flicked out my tongue to taste the pre-cum that gathered on the head. He groaned and pushed deep into my mouth in response. Joshua grabbed my hands, cuffed my wrists with one of his hands above my head, and started to work his cock in and out of my mouth with sure, steady strokes. Each push inside sent a little shiver of need straight to my clit. I twisted beneath him, desperate for more but determined to please him at the same time.

"Fuck." He paused and then carefully pulled away. "Don't move."

I relaxed on the bed and watched through half-closed eyes as he pulled a condom from the box and tore open the wrapper. When he moved over me, I spread my legs wide for his body. Joshua penetrated with one long, sure thrust and when he was buried to the hilt he stopped and covered my mouth with his.

The lazy thrust of his tongue into my mouth was a harsh contrast with the thick invasion of his cock. The walls of my cunt clenched around him and when he started to move, I lifted my hips to meet him. I clutched at his back, my nails scoring his damp skin.

He pulled his mouth from mine, clutching my hips in a tight grip as he moved to his knees. The penetration changed, deepened, and the rawness of it stoked the need that brewed between us both until he was slamming into me ruthlessly. I took each pounding thrust gratefully and when he lifted my legs up onto his shoulders I shuddered in acceptance.

Completely at his mercy, I watched as he worked his cock in and out of my pussy, each inward thrust accompanied by the sound of skin smacking together and the thud of his balls slapping my ass. His fingers dug into my hips hard, his short, neatly manicured nails hard against my skin, and I could almost feel the bruises I would sport later for that sharp little pleasure.

"Come." He demanded through clenched teeth. "Come now."

I wanted it so bad I could taste it. My body was building toward something so hard and mean that I could barely stand to think about it. His fingers caught my clit, pinched, and I came in one vicious rush screaming his name. He let my legs fall from his shoulders and then he thrust against me one last time.

Joshua lowered us both to the bed and rested on me, his forehead flush with mine. Our bodies were fluid and relaxed as the pleasure of orgasm slipped away. I ran one hand down his back and sighed when he moved away and pulled free. Suppressing a frown, I watched him roll from the bed and disappear into the bathroom.

When he returned, he stopped at the edge of the bed and looked me over with a critical eye. "I wasn't too rough with you?"

"No. Not at all." I stretched and smiled in an effort to put him at ease. "We should probably shower and get dressed. I'm more than sure Kristen will be calling me any minute now asking if we should meet to discuss your latest little thing."

He sighed. "Am I that much of a hassle?"

"Hassle?" I glanced him over, taking in his leanly muscled body and still nearly erect cock while trying not to appear as if I were inspecting him. "No, not normally. Other than the skinny-dipping, the parties where the women outnumber the men three to one that last all night long, the bar fights . . ."

"Oh, come on. I haven't had a fight in a bar in literally two years."

"It's still something we battle against. Your reputation preceded you into Atlanta and that's not necessarily a bad thing considering recent events." I rolled out of the bed and stretched. "And as you said, you've been a very good boy this year."

He raised one eyebrow. "Boy? I don't remember calling myself a boy."

The word hardly did him justice, but seeing his eyes harden in challenge was fun. "Principle is the same."

"Woman, I thought you said you wanted to shower and get dressed."

"That's my plan."

"Keep talking shit to me and you'll find yourself all tied up and unavailable when your friend calls." He disappeared into the bathroom. "You'll be lucky if I play with you after I tie you up."

I figured my luck was pretty good but I kept my expression cool and innocent as I followed along behind him. "We actually do have work to do."

"Yeah, yeah."

3

I filled my coffee cup and took a sip as Kristen arranged her laptop on my kitchen table. Joshua was leaning against one of the counters with a bottle of water looking fresh and all sparkly as if he hadn't just fucked me for two hours. I'm sure I looked like a dog in need of a good grooming. I grabbed a mug for Kristen, filled it, and set it on the table as the doorbell rang.

I waved Joshua off and went to answer it myself, just in case it wasn't Sonya. The last thing I needed was some too-eager-for-their-own-good reporter finding Joshua at my apartment. I threw open the door and motioned Sonya inside. She hauled in her computer without a word and went into the kitchen.

My small kitchen had served as our war room more times than I could count, long before we could afford really nice office space and sometimes even now, since it offered comfort in times of extreme stress. Sonya offered Joshua a friendly salute as she sat down at the table and pulled out her computer.

As I walked by, she confiscated my coffee. Her lack of germ fear really freaked me out, but since I knew I wouldn't ask for the cup back, I went and found another.

"Okay, most of the major news networks have picked it up because it hit the AP like a hurricane an hour after it showed up on the Internet." Kristen glanced at Joshua and then focused on him. With a small frown, she continued. "I've got a friend at Fox who indicated that the two women have already agreed to interview for a tabloid show. An exclusive—which means no legitimate reporter is going to get near them any time soon."

I glared at him. "Great."

"I can't control what they say." He shrugged. "I've told you what they'll probably say but you and I both know they can make up all kinds of crap and insinuate that I'm the reincarnation of the Marquis de Sade. People will either believe them or not." He fisted his hands and then shoved them into the pockets of his slacks in frustration.

I figured he had a whole lot to say but didn't want to continue in front of Sonya and Kristen. His cell phone started to ring and, after a brief check of the caller ID, he answered it and walked out of the room. I looked toward Kristen. "Anything else?"

Sonya and Kristen shared a glance and then focused on me as if they were one person. Kristen picked up her coffee and sat back in the chair. "You tell us."

"What?"

"You both look fresh from the shower and I figured he'd be gone when I got here. He's been here for about three hours."

"Yeah, he's hiding from the press."

"In your shower?" Sonya asked and just grinned when I glared at her. "Just askin'."

"Business, please." I pinched the bridge of my nose. "Statements?"

Kristen went back to her laptop. "I'm fond of 'no comment' and 'Mr. Keller prefers not to answer questions regarding his sexuality.'"

"No." Sonya shook her head. "That last one will bring us right back to that metrosexual thing, which still stuns me what with all the women that have paraded in and out of his life in the past six or so years."

"Yeah." Now I was among them. I sucked in my bottom lip. The thought was a little unnerving to say the least.

"What about that woman he was dating? The one who practically gnawed my head off last month on the set of that shoe commercial?" Kristen grimaced as she said it. "The frigid-looking blonde."

"I dumped her." Joshua leaned against the doorway and frowned. "I'm sorry she was rude to you."

Kristen waved it off. "The day I let a bony little witch like her get the best of me is the day I quit this business and go teach kindergarten."

"Was that Gary?"

"Yes, he's unhappy since he's yet to grab Snow White's ass but he's on his way back." He tossed his cell phone onto the counter. "His wife will never bake me cookies again. I heard her shouting it in the background—which sucks because her cookies are excellent."

"As much money as you make her husband I'm sure she'll make you some more cookies." I pulled out a chair and sat down across from Sonya, and blinked just once at the feel of the wood against my thighs and back. I glanced his way and he gave me a quick grin. He knew exactly how my skin was tingling and warming against the pressure of the chair. "Now, the twin thing has totally solved the metrosexual issue."

"Oh, Christ, no one is allowed to say that word around me again." He tipped back the water bottle, drank deeply, and then encompassed all three of us in a glare. "If I have to spend the next bloody year in strip joints I will."

"No need." Sonya grinned. "As she said, the twins totally fixed that for you." She wiggled her eyebrows. "So what are our chances of a sex tape?"

I lowered my head to the table without a word while Joshua laughed. "Pretty slim. I've never taped myself and I keep all of my windows covered at home. While I was a regular patron of the Playground when I first moved here, I've never used one of their voyeur rooms and I've never engaged in a sex act on the club's premises, not even in one of the private rooms."

Kristen flushed, her pretty, pale complexion going pink. "What happens in *voyeur* rooms?"

I lifted my head and nearly laughed at his slack-jawed expression. "Yeah, Mr. Keller, what happens in those voyeur rooms?"

He cleared his throat, offering me a quick glare. "Well, voyeur rooms normally have a window or sometimes an entire wall made out of glass so that others may watch anyone in the room engage in sex or play."

"Oh." Her mouth formed a perfect O and then she focused her attention on her computer. "That's . . . wow . . . I mean . . . but you've never done that?"

"No. I find exhibitionism somewhat disturbing. I rarely watch others either. It's not my thing."

"So the ex-girlfriend?" Sonya cleared her throat. "What might she say about you if she were interviewed?"

"Stephie is a lawyer. It would probably be best for her career if she denies we had anything more than a few dates. She'll probably tell everyone she dumped me for my proclivities." He shrugged. "As it stands, I don't kiss and tell."

"Did she have a problem with your *preferences*?" I asked softly.

"Not at all."

I nodded. "Then she'll likely keep her mouth shut. A woman trying to make partner in a law firm isn't going to let on that

DANGEROUS PLAY

she likes to get . . ." I glanced at Sonya and Kristen, who were both staring at me with keen interest. "She'll be quiet. I doubt she'll be an issue. We should ignore any questions about her and play down their relationship as much as possible."

"The owner of the Playground has refused to answer questions," Sonya murmured as she continued to flip through her research. "It's free publicity for him so I'm surprised."

"A man like him doesn't run the kind of business he runs without learning to be discreet," Joshua responded. "He talks about one patron and half of his patrons disappear."

"What about the team?" Sonya asked.

"I wouldn't be the only member of my team to frequent such an establishment, and I already explained to Tara that I doubt the team owner will make it an issue. He paid through the nose to get me and this has no bearing on my ability to play the game. It's not like taking two women home from a sex club and fucking them is a crime."

Sonya sprayed coffee all over her laptop screen and Kristen covered her face with both hands. I grabbed some paper towels for Sonya and just shook my head at him. "Joshua."

"Sorry, ladies."

"Yeah, right," Sonya muttered as she dabbed at her baby. "This laptop is new, you know."

"Then you'd best not spit coffee on it again." I took her cup away, laughed when she stuck her tongue out at me, and then looked toward Joshua. "Now, have you remembered their names?"

"Hell, no." He frowned. "I'm not even sure I got their real names. They were 'strays,' Tara. I imagine they are regulars in the scene . . . at least they were. If they go on national television and discuss me I imagine they'll have a problem finding a man who will top them in this city. Discretion is a part of the lifestyle and the lack thereof is a serious breach of ethics."

37

"Top? Stray?" Kristen repeated and then frowned. "Wait, never mind; I don't want to know."

Joshua chuckled. "Your innocence is charming, Ms. Travis." He picked up his cell phone and glanced toward me. "See me out, will you?"

I followed him with a frown. "You don't want to stay and go over the press release with us?"

He turned as he reached the door and with gentle finger-tips touched my cheek. "No, I trust you."

I glanced back toward the kitchen and shook my head. "How many times have I told you that you should really play a more active role in the image that is presented?"

He leaned in and placed a soft kiss on my mouth and then on my jaw, and then moved down to my neck where he nipped gently. "If you do something I don't like I'll just have to punish you."

A shiver of pure anticipation ran down the length of my back. "Don't tempt me."

He lifted away from me and took a step back. "I'm sure Gary will be landing within a few hours and he'll want to meet with you tomorrow at your office. That's soon enough to release a statement."

"Damage control is about timing."

"Then I trust you to do what is best and we'll deal with the rest as it comes." He brushed my hair back from my forehead. "I have some pretty filthy plans for you, Tara. I hope I won't be disappointed tomorrow."

"Regret is for pansies."

"Good." He pressed one final hard kiss against my lips and slipped out the door.

I locked it and with a frown returned to the kitchen where I knew I was about to face what one might call a Mint Julep In-quisition. Southern women were some of the nosiest bitches on the planet and I had two in my kitchen that knew *almost* everything there was to know about me.

The computers were gone off the table and a bottle of wine sat in the middle, three glass already out and full. With a sigh I sat down, picked up my glass, and drank half the contents in one crude swallow. "Did you finish the press release?"

Kristen snorted. "First, what the hell does 'top' mean?"

"It can mean a variety of things but he was referring to the dominant role in a D/s scene or relationship." I set the glass down in front of me. "But it can just mean the more aggressive partner in a relationship."

"Okay." Her dark brown eyes focused on my face as she drank from her wineglass. When she swallowed, she pursed her lips. "And?"

"And what?"

"Come on." Sonya laughed. "You were both fresh from a shower and you've got afterglow at a level I've never seen in my life. I bet you'd glow in the dark."

It had been a very satisfying encounter. "You know that I don't get involved with clients."

"Yeah, because the only one you've ever wanted hadn't made a move . . . until today." Sonya shook her head when I started to protest. "I thought we were friends."

I held up one hand in surrender and finished off my wine. "The two of you are the best friends I have in this world. I trust you with practically everything I have. My business, my reputation, my future. That being said, I'm just not ready to talk about this—at all."

We sat in silence while they adjusted to that and I refilled my glass. The situation was complicated enough without having to deal with their questions about a part of my life and my past that they knew nothing about. I figured Sonya might find my little fetish amusing or even interesting, but Kristen had often surprised me in the past. When it came to sex, she could be something of a prude. Even if she never said a word, I figured if it fucked with her head it would be written all over her face.

"We need to contact the ex-girlfriend and prepare her for press questions," I said. "If she'll play along and keep with our party line it will be for the best. Since she is a lawyer, we can hope she'll be smart enough to keep her mouth mostly shut."

"Why did he dump her?" Sonya asked softly. "I mean, if she played his games—and it appears she did—what made him shake her loose?"

That was a sobering question. I reached out and grabbed the bottle. "She started hinting that she wanted to marry his checkbook."

"Ouch."

"Yeah."

"Well, that cunt," Kristen muttered. "I should call her and tell her . . ." She paused and raised one eyebrow. "What?"

I cleared my throat, aware that I must have looked as shocked as I felt. "I don't think I've ever heard you use the word *cunt* in our lives and I've known you since we were twelve."

"Well, maybe I'm broadening my horizons." She grabbed the bottle, topped off her glass, drank deeply, and then said, "She *is* a cunt."

"She sure is." But I figured my opinion on the ex-girlfriend of my very new lover was somewhat biased.

4

The press release had done little to stave off the nightmarish press coverage, though every single newscast I watched did manage to repeat most of it. We'd opted for a calm and firm statement indicating that Mr. Keller had never been the sort of man to discuss his relationships with women and it would be ungentlemanly of him to discuss the Monroe sisters.

Candi and Cherri Monroe. I rolled my eyes and slouched in my chair. Who the hell named their twin daughters Candi and Cherri? Did their parents expect them to grow up and be strippers or something? The thought boggled my mind but I tried really hard not to dwell on it.

Our open-space office had always been a source of energy and fun. Now we were all three just staring out into space waiting on Joshua and his agent. Well, I was waiting on Joshua and his agent. I was fairly sure that Sonya and Kristen were nursing hangovers and trying to move as little as possible. We'd all gotten a little toasted but morning afters had never been a problem for me.

"So far no one is admitting to releasing the video."

I glanced at Sonya, who had four different monitors on her desk and every one of them was moving and twisting with some different Web site. She was our Internet guru and had pulled off many a fascinating thing in the past, but so far she'd had zero luck finding out where the video had started.

"So the copy on that video site?"

"There are like two hundred copies on that video site, some set to some seriously hot music. Watching him walk around in leather pants to the tune of 'Closer' by Nine Inch Nails adds a fine edge of nasty to the whole thing."

I pursed my lips and turned in my chair to look out our window. I had a *stunningly* boring view of the building across the street and practically every office on the same level with us. Most of them had their blinds drawn against the morning sun.

The elevator dinged and I stood as Joshua and his agent left the car. Gary offered a wide grin and a set of open arms.

"How are my favorite ladies?"

"Grab her ass, Gary, and I'll break your hand," Joshua muttered as he followed his agent toward my desk.

I laughed as Gary did, in fact, get a hug in. "Gary, how was your vacation?"

"A nightmare. I was so glad to have a reason to come home. The damn wife had a 'plan' and every minute of the trip was to be executed with precision or we all paid the price. I felt bad leaving my kids, but at that point it was every man for himself." He winked and took a seat in one of the chairs in front of my desk. "Now, about my boy and the trouble . . ."

Joshua sighed and took a seat beside him. "The team owner called and basically wants me to get interviewed so I can categorically deny being involved in the sex club."

I pursed my lips. "I see. Why?"

"His wife is offended and embarrassed."

"Okay." I rubbed the bridge of my nose and glanced toward

Kristen, who was still working on our response to the Associated Press. "First, I would prefer that you *not* get on television and lie. Lies come back to bite and bites like that get infected and things have to be amputated."

"He reminded me that the contract has a morality clause."

"And you can remind him that your contract also has a hefty compensation package for early termination or breach." I picked up the contract in question and waved it. "He might not remember it but I'm sure Gary won't have a problem reminding him. If he can't play ball and walk our party line then maybe he'd prefer to pay you for the next three years while you play for someone else."

Gary laughed and clapped his hands. "That's why I love these women."

I decided that I wouldn't mention the fact that Gary had fought hiring a "bunch of broads" for publicity when Joshua had first come to The Marcus Group for representation. "I realize that you like and respect the man but that doesn't mean we're going to roll over and let him dictate such a thing. It would, in fact, be a violation of your morality clause to go on television and tell a big fat lie."

"Yes." He ran his fingers through his hair and slouched back in the chair in defeat. "But I doubt she's the only woman in town who feels this way. How do we smooth that over?"

"I have a plan." Gary glanced at his watch and then grinned when the elevator sounded again. "It's perfect, really."

Stephie Wilson sashayed off the elevator. The effort it took for me to not scream like a banshee could not be measured by any scale invented by man. She offered us all a fake little smile and I gifted it right back to her. "Ms. Wilson, this is a private office space and we're in the middle of a meeting. I thought I made it pretty clear what we expected from you when you and I spoke earlier."

"Yes. I know." She went to the chair right beside Joshua and sat down. "Gary suggested I attend. I've already released my own statement to the media."

Joshua jerked upright in the chair and pulled his hand away when she tried to grab it. "Gary?"

"Stephie called me this morning and offered to help with our little problem." Gary glanced toward the woman and smiled broadly. "I think she's the perfect solution."

I was positive the whole damn thing was about to turn into the sort of scene that could put a person in a mental institution. "What did you say to the press?"

She sniffed as if she wasn't in the mood to talk to me and focused on Joshua. "I told them that you only visited that awful club because we'd had some problems in our relationship but that everything was better now that we were engaged."

I'd never seen fury born before. But it blossomed on Joshua's face with all good speed and Gary bolted up from his chair as if he'd been stuck in the ass with a sword. "You what? You never said you were going to claim you two were getting married!"

I stood from my chair and swallowed hard. "Sonya, would you get Mr. Keller a bottle of water? He looks like he could use a break."

"Don't handle me." The softly spoken words brought everyone in the room to a standstill. It was the moment I'd been waiting for, the hard edge to his voice and the attempt at rearranging our working relationship. "Stephie, I didn't agree to your participation in this situation and I'm certain I made myself perfectly clear three months ago that I was finished with you."

"But, Joshua darlin', surely you understand that now you need someone like me." She touched his arm, her big, pretty blue eyes wide with pretended innocence. "I'm the perfect solution to your problem. I go to a good church, I'm a professional career-minded woman, and no one would think for a minute that I'd indulge in such a lifestyle with you. With me on your arm, the rumors will die fast."

"I said no." He stood and walked to stand in front of the window behind my desk.

She tucked her overpriced handbag under her arm as she got up from the chair. "You'll change your mind. I think things will only get worse for you."

I watched her stalk out of the room and then shared a glance with Sonya, who had paused in her searching to watch the show. "We must find out where the video came from and start running automatic searches on his name every minute. I want to know immediately when the next *thing* hits."

Joshua leaned forward and rested his forehead against the glass. "Did she release the video?"

"Did you know her last year?"

"I'd seen her at the club a few times in the summer but there had been nothing personal or sexual between us. We met again at a party and started dating then."

"So she could have been in the position to take that cellphone video," Sonya cued the video up and watched it on the big center monitor that dominated her desk space. "The person taking this footage is only a few feet from you and they are moving with the flow of the crowd leaving the club. So it was someone who followed you out."

I walked to her desk and motioned her to play it again. "Okay, so what else might she have?"

"It would depend on how comfortable she was in his home or if he ever spent the night with her." Sonya glanced around me with a raised eyebrow. "Have you?"

He was leaning on the edge of my desk when I turned to look at him. "I prefer my own home for such things. Privacy is important."

"So it's unlikely that she's recorded you, say, in a bedroom setting."

His mouth curved into a grin. "If you want to watch me have sex, Ms. Carson, why don't you just ask?"

Sonya laughed and went back to the computer. "It could just be more of this stuff. We won't know until the next bomb drops, and from her attitude when she left I believe it will be soon."

If it was her, yes, it would be soon. I cleared my throat. "I'm thinking maybe we should decline to comment on the engagement thing. It might work in your favor for the time being."

"Absolutely not." He glared at me as if I'd suggested he put on a dress. "I want an immediate statement released saying that she and I haven't been a couple in several months and that there is no engagement."

"I'd like to speak with Mr. Keller alone, please." I hoped my tone of voice was even, because I felt like I might explode at any moment.

Kristen hopped up from her desk and grabbed her purse. "Hey, Gary, why don't you buy me a coffee?"

Sonya offered me a glare but abandoned her computer to walk with Kristen and Gary to the elevator.

When the doors closed on them Joshua let out a sigh. "Fuck. Fuck. Fuck."

"Yes, something like that. I can't protect you if you let Gary do whatever the hell he wants," I ground out between clenched teeth. I wanted to scream at him; to remind him that I wasn't someone he could order around in the light of day.

"Gary has been with me a long time. Far longer than you have." His lips pressed together in a thin line.

"And he encouraged your ex-girlfriend to inject herself into this situation without discussing it with you or with me."

"And last night I was thinking to protect her from this mess." He rubbed his mouth with one hand and then sat back down in the chair he'd abandoned. "I didn't want to answer the question in front of the others, but I'm pretty damn sure I gave her the opportunity to record us in a sexual act. I spent plenty of time at her apartment and in her bed in the three months we dated."

"Anything hardcore?"

"Probably. She has a thing for Shibari and anal sex."

I raised one eyebrow. Japanese rope bondage had always been a little extreme for me. That much immobilization required so much trust and I rarely gave anyone who topped me that kind of physical control over my body. "Okay, but considering the offer she made today she wouldn't release anything that would put her in such a light. Did she ever ask you for something light and romantic? A different kind of scene than you normally played? Straight sex, no toys or bondage—something very intimate?"

His mouth dropped open. "Fuck me."

"I take that as a yes." I slid into my desk chair. "Okay, then we'll see what she does."

"We can't stop her?"

"If she has a sex tape she probably has it all ready to be released." I glanced him over. "At least you won't have anything to be embarrassed about."

"Except a bunch of strangers watching me fuck."

"Yeah." I grimaced at the outrage on his face and the hurt he couldn't completely hide. "I'm sorry."

"It's not your fault I trusted her."

"But it is my fault you were involved with her." I held up a hand. "I was the one who suggested you go out and get a presentable girlfriend. The next thing you know the bony blonde is at your games wearing your number and bouncing around like a college girl for the press. Going to your charity events . . ."

"It was sound advice and it played well with female fans that I'd hooked up with a woman who was powerful and had her own career." He left the chair and started to pace. "She was sexy enough for men but smart enough for women to respect her."

"Why did you hire me?" Not a question I often asked of clients. I've always been arrogant enough to assume that they all hired me because I was fantastic and perfect.

"Because you were hot."

My mouth dropped open. "Pardon me?"

He shrugged and offered a small smile. "I met you at a party that one of my teammates threw. He introduced you as his PR agent and I was looking for one. Gary kept introducing me to these old guys who thought the Internet was a fad. I needed someone plugged in and ready to hit the ground running. I met you, heard you were a great agent to work with, and it was an added bonus that you were sex on two legs."

I wanted to throw something at him, but it was hard to pretend to be angry when you're ridiculously pleased. "After we signed you, we had a bevy of high-profile clients come our way, so thank you."

"I can't imagine the world of shit I would be in if you hadn't agreed to take me on as a client." He frowned. "I was pushing my limits, living life too hard, and things were starting to snag around the edges. I guess I sort of let you take over my life to avoid making my own choices."

Ouch. I winced at that, mostly because it was true. I did run his life. I picked his parties, who he had dinner with . . . and had even had some small role in picking the type of woman he dated on a long-term basis. Too bad he'd picked something of a psycho. It really didn't mesh with the sexually dominant man I now knew him to be.

"I should have paid attention to her. It's my job to protect your image, and I let someone get close to you who is obviously not pulling a full apple cart." I jotted down a note to get a full background check done on the woman and then glared at him. "Why do you hook up with women who have stupid names? Candi, Cherri, Stephie?"

He frowned. "Who are Candi and Cherri?"

"The twins."

"Oh." Joshua shrugged. "You don't have a stupid name."

I snorted. "My mother named me after the plantation in *Gone With the Wind;* trust me, that's stupid enough." I tapped my pen on the desk. "As for the team, we'll think of something reasonable for the owner and his offended wife. Perhaps you could send her flowers."

"Been there. Done that." He grinned when I raised an eyebrow. "I've pissed off enough women in my life to know how to make the first peace offering as quickly as possible. I'm going to follow it up with a day at the spa of her choice. By Friday she'll know I'm a sex fiend but she won't care."

I walked around my desk and leaned back on it. My goal was casual and confident but I wasn't entirely sure I'd pulled it off. "So, what happens when you're *finished* with me?"

He winced. "I can't believe I said that out loud. She just made me so angry."

"Oh, we could all tell. I don't know how she managed to sit there beside you." I crossed my arms over my breasts. "Answer the question."

"You said that regret was for pansies."

"I don't regret yesterday or tonight or tomorrow. I just want to know what's going to happen when you're done. On a personal level I'll be fine, but on a business level having one of my biggest clients leave for no apparent reason is going to be hard to explain."

He stood up, walked to me, and planted his hands on the desk on either side of me. "You'll be fine on a personal level?"

I laughed softly. "You aren't the first man I've taken a ride on and I'll doubt you'll be the last. I'm a big girl, Joshua; I just need to know that I'm playing with a grown man who can keep his business and his personal matters separate."

"You doubt I'll be the last?" he asked as he lowered his head. His lips trailed over the side of my neck, connected with my earlobe, and tugged. "What if I find such a thought irritating?"

"It probably won't be the last time I irritate you." I sucked in a breath as his hands rested briefly on my hips and then trailed up my back in one swift motion. "I'm not a woman known for inspiring peace in others."

"Is that so?"

"Yeah."

"I wanted to kiss you the moment I walked into this room." He brushed his lips over mine in a way that was so gentle and exploring that it made me ache all the way to my toes. "I love seeing you here, strong and in control of your world. Makes me want to bend you over this too-big desk and fuck you until you can't even think about letting another man get near what's mine."

He gave me no time to respond. His mouth covered mine in the second he finished speaking, his tongue whipping into my mouth to taste and explore. When he lifted me onto the desk, I spread my legs and made room for him between them. It seemed like the perfect thing to do regardless of our timing and location. Joshua slid his hands up my bare legs, under the hem of my skirt, and snagged the sides of my panties.

I groaned and dropped my hands to his to stop him.

He lifted his head, his eyes glittering with determination. As if to prove his point he pressed forward and let me feel the hard ridge of his cock rest against my pussy. The clothes that separated us were unbearable in that instant but it couldn't continue.

"They could return at any moment, this is my place of business, and most important the damn blinds are open. Half the building across the street can see right into this office, and I'm pretty sure one sex tape released on the Internet is enough for anyone."

He lowered his forehead to mine and sighed. "I need to call my lawyer and see if I can't get some kind of an emergency court thing going to prevent her from releasing any video footage of us in an intimate situation."

"Good idea." I leaned forward and pressed my lips against his. "Come over for dinner tonight and I'll make this up to you."

"Damn straight you will." He caught my bottom lip in his teeth and pressed. The sharp, quick little pain shot right to my already throbbing clit. Joshua plucked me off the desk and set my on my feet with obvious reluctance.

"We can play games in the bedroom, Joshua. I'm pretty sure I'll let you do anything you'd like to me when it comes to sex. I wasn't lying when I said I was a sexual submissive. I enjoy pain and I like being dominated but that does not mean I'll tolerate your disrespect of me."

"I respect you."

"You snapped at me like I was a child in front of two employees and your manager. Even when you first contracted me and you were fighting me left and right on the image plan you never spoke to me that way. If I can't trust you to treat me with courtesy and respect in public, in front of others, how on earth am I to trust you in more intimate matters?"

His mouth dropped open briefly and then he shut it with an audible click of teeth. After a deep breath, he nodded. "You're right, of course. I came in here angry and her appearance didn't soften that a bit. That isn't, however, an excuse for speaking to you so rudely. It won't happen again."

I slid away from him, walked around my desk, and dropped down into my chair. "About the engagement."

"No." He shook his head.

"Joshua."

"No. I'll play your little press games to a point, but this is where I draw the line."

I frowned at him. "You play games for a living, Joshua."

"I play *a* game for a living. A game with rules, regulations, and where practice, talent, physical prowess, and mental strength are the tools you use to win. *You* play games with people's lives and reputations all for the sake of the next advertising dollar. You are very good at your game, Tara, and I expect you to make it clear that she's a liar. I don't care how you accomplish it."

It was true but hearing him say it so bluntly was painful. He was a product and I did my level best to sell him like one at every opportunity. I had in the past and I certainly would in the future. It was, after all, the job he'd paid me for. The elevator dinged signaling Kristen and Sonya's return. I frowned when they left the elevator alone.

"Where is Gary?"

"Downstairs arranging an appointment with several lawyers," Kristen explained. "Joshua, he told me to tell you to join him when you're finished here."

He focused on me. "Are we done here?"

"Yes." I nodded.

The room was as silent as a tomb as he walked to the side door that leads to the stairs and left. Finally, when I could bear the silence no more, I stood from my chair and went into the small kitchen area of the office to make a fresh pot of coffee.

"Kristen, please prepare a statement denying any personal involvement between Stephie Carson and Joshua. Make it as clear as you can that he is both dismayed and irritated that she would insinuate that they are engaged."

"Sure, no problem."

I had a huge problem and I knew it. I'd known it would surface even before I'd consented to play with him. Joshua was the sort of man who understood boundaries, limitations, and rules. I'd altered all of those for both of us when I'd let him tie me to my own bed and fuck me blind. Now, I had to deal with the consequences of that and find some balance of power between us.

Ten calls to local reporters, television and print, left me irritated and with little space to vent. Both Kristen and Sonya were in the same boat and bitching to the bitchy never quite satisfied. Clutching my recently purchased iced coffee, I slid into my car and began my trek home. An hour in traffic was the norm for me, and for once in a very long time I resented every single person on the road. I had a dinner to cook and a man to fuck sideways; I didn't have time to sit in traffic with a bunch of assholes.

By the time I pulled into a free parking spot down from my building my coffee was gone and my mood had gone from simply foul to fire-breathing hound from hell. I barely had time to shower and dry my hair so I ordered food and hoped it would do. Somehow I doubted if Joshua would care if I cooked for him or if he ate Kung Pow chicken out of a paper carton.

He was ten minutes early but I managed to throw on a shirt as I rushed to the door and threw it open. "You're ear . . . what the hell are you doing here?"

Stephie glanced me over with practiced disdain and invited herself right into my apartment. "I want to talk to you about Joshua."

"I don't discuss my clients with anyone. You'll have to leave."

"Look, you and I both know that this situation with the press and that stupid sex club is going to come down on him hard. I'm his best bet for coming out on top of this situation and he owes me this." Her gaze roved over me. "Why don't you get dressed and we can talk like civilized adults?"

"Why don't you take your bony ass out of my apartment?" I waved toward the hallway.

"You don't have to be crude to me. We both have Joshua's best interests in mind. I can help."

She apparently had no idea what crude really meant if she thought I was being crude. "It would have been helpful if you'd never released the video to begin with, so don't play that little game with me."

She stared for a moment and then cleared her throat. "I didn't send out the video."

"What?"

"I didn't do it. Is that what he thinks? He thinks that I would do something like that to him? I love him." Her bottom lip trembled and that was her mistake.

"Don't. He's not here to be concerned if you start crying, so suck it up."

She glanced past me and into the hall and with a sigh I turned to watch him enter my apartment. His gaze drifted from my face to hers and tears spilled down her cheeks in a delicate fall.

"Jesus." I rolled my eyes and stalked off toward my bedroom to find some pants. "I want her out of my apartment before she ruins my appetite."

I threw myself down on my bed and stared at the ceiling. The day had been one irritation after another and I was pretty sick and tired of people showing up at my apartment unannounced. I'd left him to deal with her and I supposed I should have felt embarrassed but I'd reached a point somewhere on the way home that left me pretty much incapable of being civil to assholes.

"Did you get the food from the place down the street?"

"Yeah." I rolled my head so that I could see him. "I didn't feel like cooking."

"I didn't think you would. I was prepared to take you out."

I laughed softly. "Probably not a good idea; at least not yet. Might want to give the good citizens of Atlanta time to adjust to this new little thing."

He came into the bedroom and crawled onto the bed beside me. "The team owner *invited* me to dinner tomorrow night."

"Great."

"I'm sure going to face some kind of intervention thing—or worse, a lecture from his wife. I was hoping you'd come with me."

I rolled to my knees and slid astride him. "I thought you were a big strong man. Now I see you trying to hide behind me rather than face a woman hitting the backside of fifty so hard she probably blinks every morning when she wakes up."

"I'm not afraid of her." He ran his hands up my thighs and grinned when he found no resistance to his exploration. "But, I believe it would be in my best interests to go in with reinforcements."

I gasped as he cupped my ass and lifted his hips against me. I rubbed myself briefly on his jeans, finding the hard ridge of his cock all too tempting to ignore. "These pants have to come off."

"Yeah." He sat up and kissed my mouth. "But first we should eat. We're both going to need it."

5

The challenge of understanding him overwhelmed me as I watched him secure my ankles to the footboard of my bed. It was rare that I let a man spread me out like a buffet and tie me down but when he'd told me about his plans so casually as we finished off dinner I'd been too intrigued and too hot by it to voice a single complaint.

"Comfortable?"

"Yes, Sir." I wet my lips and forced stillness on my already overstimulated body.

He must have liked my response because a small smile drifted across his lips before he picked up the duffle bag he'd retrieved from the car and dropped it on the bed between my spread legs. Flat on my stomach, I couldn't tell exactly what he pulled out and placed beside the flogger he'd had me retrieve. I angled my head for a better view and then sighed when he stopped moving.

"Nosy girl."

I grinned and lowered my head to the mattress, forehead

pressed against the crisp cotton sheet. "Am I to be punished for curiosity?"

"You are to be punished for a great many things tonight."

Wetness gushed between my labia at the thought and I pressed against the mattress for some small relief. "I was a good girl all day, Sir."

The flogger snapped in the air once just seconds before it connected with my thighs. It struck across both and the edges wrapped around to sting in the most delicious of ways. My body bowed against the rope restraints and my nipples grew unbearably hard.

The mattress dipped as he joined me on the bed and crawled up between my legs. The tresses of the flogger trailed gently down my back. "Not so."

Joshua put the flogger on the bed beside me and I groaned with disappointment. His hands slid up my legs to stroke the globes of my ass. "You denied me what's mine."

"But . . ."

"No excuses." He rubbed gently, far too gently, and then pressed one thumb against my anus. "Everything you have belongs to me and tonight I'm going to prove it."

The promise of his thumb was to make me come on the spot. I ached to press backward. To have any part of him inside of me would have been worth the potential punishment. He lifted away and I nearly howled in frustration. His soft laugh told me he was all too aware of my needy state.

"We've yet to discuss your hard limits."

Somehow I doubted he would get anywhere near a sex practice that I would consider a hard limit. He didn't seem the sort of man to get off on anything extreme. "I'm okay with toys, oral, anal. Condoms for the last one."

"Yes, of course." His hands returned and he pressed one lubed finger into my ass without pause.

I sucked in a harsh breath at the quick, nearly painful invasion and relaxed as he withdrew gently. Then cool silicone took the place of his finger. The pressure and the penetration stole my breath in one second and then it was returned to me as what could only be an anal plug was pressed firmly into place.

"Fuck."

"Good?"

"Yes, Sir." I pressed down against the mattress and rubbed my hardened clit against the sheet. It wasn't nearly enough stimulation to get me off but it helped relieve some of the pressure that was steadily building inside of me.

"Don't move." He slapped my ass, and before the stinging pain fully registered he turned the anal plug on and it started to vibrate.

"Oh, fuck!" Eyes pressed tightly shut, I curled my fists around the ropes that bound my hands and clung for all I was worth.

I barely recognized the hot slash of the flogger as it graced my back for the first time of the evening. The second strike fell harder and I arched back against it, stunned and relieved. This man knew exactly what I needed and was, at least for the moment, prepared to give it to me.

The leather slithered and struck, each stinging bite perfect against my heated flesh. I strained against the mattress and the ropes, my body taut with arousal. At first I tried to count the strikes, tried to anticipate the next lash. But after a few minutes, I surrendered to it and lost myself in the painful pleasure he created effortlessly.

"Please." I gasped and then clenched my teeth into the bedding beneath me.

"Let it go, love. Come for me."

The leather connected with my upper thighs and the shock of the quick, even strikes thrust my body into another level of sensation. Another strike to my ass sealed my fate. I came quick and hard; cum gushed between my labia and coated my inner thighs.

"That's it; God, you're beautiful." His hand slid between my legs and he pushed two fingers deep into my cunt. The penetration was shallow, small compared to the cock I knew he had for me.

"Please." I closed my eyes and pressed my whole body against the mattress to keep from rocking back against his hand. I wanted more. I needed more.

"Please what, love?"

I bit down on my lip. I was prepared to beg for his cock if I thought I would actually get it. Selfish thought, but I've always tried to be honest with myself. "I need . . ." I shuddered as he struck, the leather strips of the flogger curled around my hip in a way that was both harsh and lovely. "I need you."

"Me, or will any cock do?" He pushed his fingers in deep, connected with my G-spot with astounding accuracy, and pressed down. "Is it really me you need?"

"Yes, please."

"Tell me what you want."

"I want you to fuck me." I cried out when he jerked his fingers free. "Please!"

Joshua pushed a pillow under me, tilted my hips, and shoved his cock into my aching pussy with one hard, bone-jarring thrust. He was still for a moment, the handle of the flogger dug into my hip from where he still held it. Full of him and what now felt like a very large anal plug, I stayed put and let my pleasure ride on the vibrations of the toy. The dual stimulation was delicious and painful all in the same moment. Joshua dropped the flogger on the bed and ran both hands up my back.

I hissed at the contact and my body rushed toward orgasm despite my determination to hold out until he was ready for me to come again. He scraped his nails over my shoulder blades and a soft moan escaped my lips. I strained against the ropes. The soft, resilient cotton rubbed against the skin on my ankles and wrists with each movement.

"Good?"

"Yes, Sir."

Slowly he withdrew and then pressed back in with the kind of exaggerated care that seemed impossible considering our positions. I wanted him to ride me, use me hard . . . until I screamed . . . until I passed out. Again, again he penetrated; each measured thrust of his body left both pleasure and agony in its wake.

He slapped my ass, hard, and I shuddered. The feeling of his skin connecting with mine was intimate and so very strange when compared with the leather of the flogger. The difference was amazing, and when he did it again, I tightened on his cock uncontrollably.

"I'm going to fuck you the way I want as long as I want . . . until you forget what it's like to be empty."

The drag of his rigid flesh in and out of my body grew more intense as seconds slid into minutes. When his hands started to slip in the fine layer of perspiration that covered my entire body, he turned off the plug and pulled it from my ass with one savage jerk. The abrupt action pushed a startled scream past my lips and it turned into a groan as he started to thrust his cock into me in quick jabs.

One hand slid under us, his fingers pushed between my slick labia and he caught my clit in a tight pinch. "Come."

My body met his demand before my mind fully registered it. The walls of my cunt tightened and flexed around him, taking each skin-slapping thrust as my body gushed with release. Slowly, I relaxed beneath him and closed my eyes as he continued. I could barely think, and I didn't care. It was a rare state for me to be in and he'd gifted it to me with the sharp bite of a flogger and very thorough fucking.

His fingers caught my clit again and he started to rub in a small circle.

"Oh, God." I buried my face against the mattress and clenched my teeth in the sheets to keep from demanding that he stop.

Joshua worked my oversensitive clit expertly. "Come, again."

I groaned when he plunged deep into me and stopped. "I can't."

He pressed against my clit with two fingers and grabbed the top of the headboard with his free hand. His teeth grazed my shoulder, nipping at the already tender flesh as he leaned over me. I pulled at the ropes that bound my ankles, overwhelmed with the need to gain some purchase, some level of control in our situation.

"Nervous?" His lips brushed over the top of my ear as he started to stroke my clit again. "How much control will you sacrifice, love?"

I clenched my teeth as my hands slipped on the ropes I gripped. My nails bit into my palms, but I barely felt it. Everything in me was focused on the press of his body on mine, the dig of ropes on my skin, his cock filling and stretching my pussy until it seemed there was no way to separate us.

"Do you understand what I want from you?"

Yes. Of course I did. But total submission didn't come easy and never had. My sexuality had always warred with my intellect and more often than not it lost. I rocked back against him, tried to pull up my knees but he pressed me back onto the bed with the weight of his body and pinched my clit. The pain of it rushed over me like the lash of a whip and I screamed as orgasm followed in its wake.

My body jerked and thrashed beyond my control, causing the ropes to tighten slightly on my wrists and ankles as he started to thrust deep and hard into me. The quick jabs of his cock into my clenching depths made his own need very clear. His teeth sank into the skin of my shoulder as he jerked and grew still. A soft groan escaped his lips as he pulled free from my body and lifted away.

"I'm not going to play games with you if you can't control yourself," Joshua admonished softly as he rubbed my wrist with gentle fingers. "It probably won't leave a mark."

I leaned back against his chest and ran one foot along his leg. "You're supposed to relax when you take a swim in a big garden bathtub."

"How exactly would you explain rope burn?"

Yeah, I had no idea how I would've explained such a thing, but the skin on my wrists and ankles was barely pink and would be fine by morning. "My daddy always said it was a mistake to borrow trouble." I took his hand and kissed his palm. "Relax and let Calgon take you away."

"I can't believe you talked me into a bubble bath." His hands slid down into the water and wrapped around my hips to pull me closer. "Are we a mistake?"

"No." *Yes. Probably.* It was hard to think with his cock rapidly hardening between the cheeks of my ass. "We're consenting adults and what we do is none of anyone's business."

"What would your coworkers think?"

"I'm pretty damn sure Sonya is banging one of our clients and Kristen has a rule about it but she has lots of rules about dating. They have no room to talk about my sexual relationships."

"Yeah, except neither one of them is hooking up with a man

who likes to tie women up and spank them." He nuzzled my neck as he cupped both breasts. Thumbs drifted lazily over my hard nipples. "Are you worried about what they would think?"

How could I not? I was the owner and operator of the business that kept us all flush and living nicer than we'd ever thought possible on our own. My image was just as important, if not more so, than the professional athletes we represented. After all, if I didn't look like I could handle my business, they wouldn't even consider letting me handle theirs. As much as I knew I was entitled to a private life, I also knew that my job made me vulnerable to the opinions of others.

"They've been my friends forever. Hell, I've known Kristen since grade school and Sonya since junior high. Do I think they would find my little fetish amusing? Absolutely. Would they turn their backs on me? No way. Could it hurt my business?" I paused and sighed. "Yes. If my male clients knew what you know about me, it would alter how they treated me. They would seek—even unintentionally—to put me into a submissive role in our business dealings. I would no longer be effective in my role as their PR agent. The vast majority of them wouldn't even take me seriously anymore."

Saying it out loud made my stomach hurt a little, but it was the truth. Allowing myself to indulge in sexual excess was a quick and sure path to disaster. I'd never participated in the *scene* and there were plenty of venues I could have gone to within the fine old city of Atlanta. The risk of running into a client or the friend of a client had been great, but that had never been what kept me away. No, I'd been afraid of losing myself in the crush of my own wants.

"So, about dinner with Harry and Livie?"

"Stupid name." I grabbed my bath sponge and started kneading it. "What grown woman allows herself to be called Livie?"

"You can ask her."

"Yeah, that'll sure put a positive spin on your situation."

The owner of the team and his wife should have been the least of my worries. They should have come down hard on their star player's side, but situations like this made for too much strife in polite society.

Joshua nuzzled my neck, his hands drifting over my body in lazy circles until one delved between my legs. "We should get some sleep."

It had occurred to me that I should ask him to leave, but as he pushed two big fingers into my pussy all rational thought leaked right out of my brain. The man was an addiction; a hot, pervy addiction that had my heart racing and my body craving more.

"Yeah. Sure. Sleep." I arched against him and sighed when he pulled his fingers free. "Don't be a tease, Joshua."

"Let's find a firm flat surface." He urged me out of the tub. "Now."

We managed to make it to the bed and tumbled onto it a tangle of limbs and damp towels that were more a hindrance than a help. With a frustrated growl, he jerked my towel from between us and fisted one hand in my hair. Thick muscled thighs wedged between my legs and he sank balls deep into my cunt without another sound. We lay straining against each other, my fingers clutched sheets beneath us, his hand clenched in my hair, and our mouths barely an inch apart.

"I thought I could take my time." His lips brushed over mine, and I groaned when he dipped his tongue inside to brush against my teeth. Joshua lifted his head. "I want to be gentle with you, make love with you, but you make it impossible."

I wanted that. I needed it as much as I wanted him hard, heavy, and demanding on top of me. I tucked my legs around his waist as he started to move and met each thrust of his hips with one of my own. Our gazes locked together as we both worked to please the other, and no matter how much I wanted to I couldn't hide from him.

His eyes darkened and he slowed down. Each measured thrust was a hot drag against the walls of my cunt and the need to come was overwhelming.

"Put your hands on me."

I let go of the sheets and ran my hands down the length of his back. He shuddered against me as I clenched my nails on his ass. "I'll do whatever you want."

"Tara." His fingers tightened in my hair as he arched in my arms, his body tight with pleasure and restraint. "Fuck."

"I love this." I ran one hand down the center of his chest, over the finely cut muscles of his stomach to the base of his cock. Sliding my fingers into the black silky hair I found there, I watched him push his cock deep into my pussy. "I love watching you fuck me."

He reached between us, grabbed my hand, and pressed my fingers against my clit. "Come for me, love."

Joshua thrust hard and deep in that moment, connecting with my G-spot, and orgasm rushed so hard and fast that I screamed. I tightened around him and shook as I released.

6

Olivia "Livie" Smyth-Reagan was just as I remembered her, and for all of her Old South snootiness, her home was lovely. Harold Reagan, aka Giant Pansy, owned Joshua's team and it was obvious he was going to do what it took to keep his little wife happy. It was really too bad he wasn't a good old boy who knew how to keep his woman in her place. No matter how horrible and sexist it was for me to even think this, it would have at least made things easier on me.

I took the glass of wine Harold offered and smiled when he told me to call him Harry. Yeah, I really couldn't. Not ever. Livie and Harry. Jesus. It couldn't have gotten any worse if he'd suggested I call him Scooter. Okay, that would have been worse. I took a seat beside Joshua on an Italian leather sofa that certainly cost more than I made in a month and offered them both a smile.

"Joshua has told me you'd like him to have a live interview and deny involvement in the club he was caught on film in."

"Yes." Harold crossed his legs and settled one arm over the

back of the couch he and his wife had retreated to. "It would be best for the team."

"No, it would make you feel better, but to have him appear on television in an interview that would very likely get national coverage and outright lie about events several hundred people witnessed would be, for lack of a better word, stupid." I leaned forward and put the wine down on a low glass table that rested between us. "More to the point, such an act on his part would make him vulnerable to the morality clause in his contract, which I think is exactly what you want. It's not going to happen."

Harold sputtered and Livie glared.

"Why did you come here if you don't agree with what I want?"

"To remind you, *Livie*, that your husband's bottom line is directly affected by the success of his team, and if things become so uncomfortable for Joshua here and he has to seek placement with another team, he'll take his signing bonus and his severance package with him. This will blow over and until it does, your husband would be better served to stand beside him and at least pretend he doesn't care."

Harold laughed. "You're your daddy remade." He finished off his wine in one long swallow and sighed. "Well, hell, son."

"I make every effort to keep my private life to myself. I believe I've done well since coming to Atlanta to keep what you might view as something negative out of the press." He leaned back against the couch and his fingers grazed my shoulder as he slid one arm behind me.

"At least it isn't a video of him tied up and taking a whip to his ass." I raised one eyebrow when Livie gave a little yelp. "So count yourself lucky that your new star likes to be on top. If it were the opposite you might have a hard time explaining it to your male fans. As it stands, he took home a set of twins and fucked them. There isn't a man in the country who doesn't 'get' that, even if he pretends otherwise for his wife or girlfriend."

"You are no lady." Livie stood but her husband grabbed her hand and jerked her back down to the sofa. "Harry, I'm finished speaking with this horrible woman."

Harold cleared his throat. "This young woman's daddy can buy and sell me ten times over and still have money to roll around naked in for the rest of his natural life. Joshua doesn't want to do the interview and Ms. Marcus is right: this will blow over."

Fuck me sideways. I hazarded a glance toward Joshua and it was immediately clear that the rich-daddy business was news to him. It wasn't something I kept a secret, but I didn't make it habit to put my business in the streets either.

"My father has nothing to do with this."

"Yes, yes, of course."

Harry waved his hand as if he accepted it but I had a feeling my mere presence in his home made him feel threatened. It was an irritating development.

I stood. "I believe our business is finished, and we will leave you in peace."

"Stay for dinner," Harold offered as he stood.

I glanced toward his wife and shook my head. "Despite what she might think, I'm not about to make your wife uncomfortable in her own home for an extended period of time. We'll take our leave."

We made it all the way outside and into his car before Joshua spoke again. He turned the key in the ignition and the car woke with a purr, a soft tribute to German engineering. The sleek little BMW was his pride and joy, and it had been the first thing he'd purchased when he'd come to Atlanta.

"Your father is Andrew Marcus."

"Yes."

"And you didn't see fit to tell me?" He reached over, pulled my seatbelt over my lap, and secured me in the seat as if it were a task he did often.

I settled back in the seat and considered my words. "It's not often I *have* to tell anyone who my father is."

"Yeah, I get that. I don't know why I never made the connection."

I swallowed back a sigh and looked out the window as he put the car in motion. It had been a long damn time since I'd apologized for who I was or where I'd come from. Granted, I'd come from a lot of money but I made my own way in the world. I *could* have lived off my father for my entire life. Several of my siblings did and were perfectly content to dart around the world on his dime. I chose to leave his money alone and, while he'd helped me secure my first business loan, I had earned every penny that had gone into The Marcus Group.

I plucked my phone from my purse and browsed my in-box in the silence of the car. The subject of the newest e-mail message made me groan. "Fuck."

"What?"

"Part two of our little disaster has begun." I opened the message and then frowned. "What the hell?"

"If that bitch has released . . ."

"No. It's not a new video." I closed the message and immediately dialed Kristen. "Explain."

Kristen took a deep breath and sighed. "You'll have to come here."

"Okay. On my way." I disconnected the phone. "I need to go back to the office."

Kristen was at her desk, her dark hair tumbled around her shoulders, her eyes wet with tears. Sonya was at her work station working silently. Her expression spoke volumes about her mental state. I tossed my purse onto my desk and leaned against it. Joshua had been displeased to be left in the car but I had to hear it on my own first. I'd asked him to give us ten minutes.

"Talk to me."

Kristen shrugged and then bit down on her lip. "The reporter caught me off guard. It's no excuse, I know that."

"Did she mention me specifically at the start?"

"Yes."

"Tell me exactly what she said."

"I was picking up my dry cleaning. She caught me coming out and asked me about Joshua. I told her no comment. Then she asked me about you and your relationship with him. Then she produced pictures of the two of you in this office." She flushed. "You were sitting on the desk and both of his hands were up your skirt."

"Fuck me."

"Yes, that's exactly what it looked like he was about to do." She plucked a Kleenex from the box on her desk and then motioned toward a folder she had in front of her. "I took the pictures and refused to return them. But she laughed it off; I imagine they are digital." Her gaze darted to the windows. All of the blinds were closed. "What the hell were you thinking, Tara?"

Yeah, I deserved that and a lot more. "For which part? Fucking our biggest client or for getting momentarily so wrapped up in him I forgot where we were?"

Sonya whipped around in her chair and leveled her gaze on me. "That's as far as it went, right?"

"On the desk? In this room? Yes, of course."

"It gets worse. The ex-girlfriend is claiming that you broke up their relationship, that you view our client list as some sort of private sex supply, and that you must be willing to do things for him that she never would." Sonya pursed her lips in distaste. "I've already contacted our lawyer about her public statements and your father has called your private line four times in the past twenty minutes."

"How many pictures have been released?"

"Just the two. One close up of a very passionate kiss and the other of the two of you in a position that looks very sexual." Kristen sighed. "And there is my statement."

"Which was what, exactly?"

Kristen groaned. "'I'm not in a position to comment on my employer's sex life.'"

It was an admission of sorts, something I would have probably avoided if given a choice. The pictures were damning but evidence of that sort could be doctored and altered to suit the needs of almost anyone. It would have been easy to at least insinuate that the pictures were faked. But pictures and a statement combined made for an entirely different situation.

"You spoke the truth."

"I made a stupid mistake. I know better."

Yes. She certainly did but it wasn't her fault and I couldn't let her sit there and make herself miserable over something that had little to do with her. "It's not your fault. I'm the one in pictures with him and I was most certainly the one in bed with him."

Kristen glanced toward Sonya and then cleared her throat. "So, you *like* that bondage stuff?"

It was something of an understatement and I was momentarily saved from answering it when the elevator activated. We listened to it leave our floor and I figured Joshua would be joining us soon. I cleared my throat. "We find that we are compatible in that area."

Sonya snorted. "I bet."

"Ass."

Kristen laughed softly and then shook her head. "I'm sorry that I messed up."

The elevator doors opened and Joshua exited. It would have been good if I could have apologized in kind but I didn't regret a single moment of him and doubted that I ever could.

"Show me." He shoved his hands into his pockets as he came to a stop near my desk.

Reluctantly, I walked to Kristen's desk and retrieved the folder with the pictures she'd taken from the reporter. I figured he was going to have a meltdown once he realized what was in it. I laid it down on my desk, flipped it open, and sorted the two pictures so he could view both.

He looked at the pictures for a solid minute in silence and then cleared his throat. "I apologize, love, this is"—his lips tightened into a thin line—"bloody unacceptable."

"It is what it is." I closed the folder. "It's less damaging to you than the footage at the BDSM club. If anything, it makes it clear that you're just a man being a man."

"And you? What does this do to you?"

I flushed and glanced toward Sonya and Kristen. "I honestly haven't a clue. The biggest problem is your psycho ex-girlfriend. She's all but called me a whore and insinuated that I fuck all of my clients and that I *stole* you from her."

"She was a distraction then and she's far less to me now."

"Ouch," Sonya said out loud and then blushed when he looked at her. "If a man called me a distraction I'd be pretty upset."

"I hardly think I ever called her that to her face." He didn't seem so sure but I decided to leave that alone for now. "And I doubt you'd ever have a worry about a man considering you such a thing."

"How do we work this?"

"Have you ever been in the Playground?" Kristen asked softly.

"No," I said.

"Does anyone know . . ." She flushed. "Well, hell."

"No one that would want to be involved in this mess themselves." None of the men I had dated in the past, not even the one that had called me a dyke, would risk that kind of negative media exposure.

"Stephie released the video." He closed the folder. "She had me followed and had these pictures taken."

"It's an assumption but one could certainly draw those conclusions."

"So, I made you a target." Joshua tapped the folder gently. "And now she's calling you a whore whenever a reporter looks her way."

I walked away from him, turned back on the whole room as I considered it. My phone rang and I glanced at it briefly. "Let my voicemail get it."

"It's your father again. You know if you don't talk to him soon he'll start buying things, like newspapers, and firing people, like the reporter who broke this story."

"Yes. I know." It was how my daddy dealt with things. He'd made it his goal in life to make things pleasant, and when things got unpleasant, he bought them and disposed of them as efficiently as possible. "I just don't know what to tell him."

I really didn't know what to tell anyone. For all the maneuvering I did for other people, I never expected to have to work the media on my own behalf. Stupid, reckless behavior had never been a problem for me. Being the only daughter of one of the richest men in the country had taught me early on the value of keeping my private life as private as possible.

I jerked when my phone started to ring again. With a sigh, I walked across the room and answered it. "Marcus Group, this is Tara Marcus."

"I'm in Savannah. Do I need to come home to deal with this?"

I winced at the tone and dropped into my desk chair. "It's nice to hear from you, Daddy. I'm fine. How are things going?"

"Don't be flippant, Tara Eileen, I've no time for such things."

I was dangerously close to a "poor little rich girl tantrum" and that made me feel stupid. "I'm fine, and no, I don't believe you need to come home. Why didn't you call my cell phone?"

"Because you run a business and your business is being threatened; no daughter of mine wouldn't be at the helm managing the crisis." He cleared his throat. "Are the pictures real?"

"Yes."

"He is a good man?"

"Would I have any less?"

"No." He laughed. "The bondage club?"

"Just media hype." Yeah, honesty with my father only goes so far.

"This ex-girlfriend business?"

"I think she's mental." I winced and glanced toward Joshua. "But I've learned that a man *can* make a woman crazy."

Joshua flashed me a small smile and then walked away from the desk. I relaxed in my chair as I listened to my father breathe. I knew he was preparing his next volley of questions—in an attempt to find some reason for him to come home and stick both of his big feet into my mess.

"I'll want to meet this young man when I come home."

I frowned. "What?"

"I think I have a right to meet the man who's more familiar with the underside of your skirt than Victoria's Secret."

"Daddy!" I jerked up from my slumped position, my face heating. I must have been the most unattractive shade of red. "That is . . ."

"Besides, any man who can distract you like that at work is

75

worth meeting and having a beer with." He laughed, apparently amused with himself, and I was at an absolute loss for words.

I cleared my throat and looked toward Joshua, who was looking at me intently. "I have to go. My office is full of people."

"Just let me know if you need me or my money."

I flushed. "I always need you, Daddy. Your money means very little."

"I know, baby girl. I know, and that's why it's so easy to offer it to you. Don't let that snotty, hardly educated reporter get the best of my little girl; I doubt I'd recover from the embarrassment."

"Hardly educated?"

"You'll find a report about her in your e-mail."

I was still trying to close my mouth when I realized he'd hung up on me. With a disgruntled sigh, I put the phone back in the receiver and looked at my computer monitor. The screen saver was active, and for a few seconds I just stared at the artificial fish swimming around in their bright blue virtual aquarium. I suppose some computer programmer thought it would be relaxing. I'd never found it to be. In fact, the busy little fish often made me fidget.

"What?" Sonya asked.

I jerked my gaze from the computer to Sonya. "My father had a background check done on the reporter who broke the story."

Sonya grinned. "That's why I like your daddy. Lucky for him he goes through women like socks or I might give him a spin."

I glared at her. "I thought we agreed you couldn't sleep with my father."

"Yeah, yeah." She waved me off. "Check the file."

I reached out, snagged my mouse, and the screen saver blinked away. Locating the e-mail wasn't a problem, and I opened it. The attached file was large and probably contained information

I'd rather not know about a woman who was sticking her nose into my business.

I opened it with a small sigh and frowned. "We went to college with her."

"No way, I'd have recognized her." Kristen hopped up from her chair and walked to my desk. Hands on her hips, she stared at the picture for a full thirty seconds before she made a sound. "That's Jeannie Purdell."

"Looks like she goes by Jean Turst now."

"Purdell?" Sonya asked. She stood up and came over to the computer. "That snotty girl who wouldn't give us the time of day and made up that rumor about Kristen sleeping with a professor senior year?"

"Yeah, that one." I closed the report and forwarded it to both of their e-mail accounts. "We need to find out all we can about what Jeannie has been up to and then I want to meet with her."

7

"Do you think it's a good idea to meet with this reporter?"

I glanced toward Joshua as we left the elevator and headed toward his car. "Yes. She sought out one of my employees on her personal time and grilled her about my personal life. Since she's made no attempt whatsoever to contact me, I get the feeling she's not really interested in getting answers. That makes this story and her involvement personal and I want to know what I did to her to warrant it."

"How does this connect to me, the video, or Stephie?" He opened up the passenger door.

I slid into the seat and got comfortable while he went around the car. When he was settled behind the wheel I answered his question. "You're a high-profile client for my firm and maybe that video surfaced not because of you but because of me. Stephie did deny sending it out."

"And you think she'll just spill her guts if you ask?"

"I think I'll know for certain what I'm dealing with after I talk to Jean."

The ride to my apartment was done in silence but I wasn't

comforted by it. If this was all about me, someone from my past had messed with his reputation and his career. He had every right to be pissed and I figured he was trying to find a way to tell me that he was going to put some distance between us professionally and personally.

He parked on the curb and turned the car off. "Can I come up or would that just add fuel to the fire?"

I laughed softly, relieved at his dry, almost bored tone. "At this point, I don't care."

There was a man sitting on the floor in front of my apartment with a laptop balanced on his legs. I hadn't had a reporter waiting at my door in a very long time, perhaps since the last time my father had gotten divorced. In fact, it was the same reporter.

"I thought I told you to never darken my door again." I put both hands on my hips in mock ire.

Cord Phillips offered me a grin. "Your daddy said you might like a friendly reporter to talk to."

I rolled my eyes at the irony and focused on Joshua. "Do you mind?"

"Do what you need. I'm not going anywhere, love."

Cord rolled to his feet. "Can I quote him on that?"

"No, you may not." I glared at him. "I mean it."

He raised his free hand. "Okay, okay. Look, I'm here because your 'too rich for his own good' father is good friends with my boss. I agreed to do it as long as I can be honest but I know when to keep something off the record." He held out his hand to Joshua. "Cord Phillips, Jr."

"I'd say it was a pleasure to meet you"—Joshua took his hand—"but I hate reporters."

Cord grinned. "Yeah, we're pretty horrible to you guys in general. Come on, then; I bite but I've had all my shots."

I dug my keys from my purse and unlocked the door. "Do you know Jean Turst?"

"Yeah, but I call her by a special pet name."

"Oh, yeah?"

"Wicked Witch of the South." He moved into my living room without an invitation and opened his laptop. "Plug?"

I motioned toward a wall outlet behind him. "Just make yourself at home."

Joshua tossed his jacket across the back of the couch and went toward the kitchen. "Wine?"

"A thousand times, yes." I pinched the bridge of my nose as I sat down on the couch. "Cord."

"Yeah?"

"They didn't threaten your job?"

"No."

"Good." I relaxed against my couch.

"Your father can be pushy but I've never known him to be dishonest. I mean, he has a reputation for protecting his own but he wouldn't have talked my boss into sending me your way if he didn't expect it would do more good than harm. You would have told me to fuck off if you hadn't agreed with him."

It irked me that my father hadn't mentioned his little interference, but since I would have avoided home altogether if I'd known, I figured he knew me pretty well. It was a smart move, just not one I truly wanted to endure.

Joshua pressed a glass of wine into my hand and then got comfortable on the couch beside me. I was torn between keeping him around for comfort and sending him back to the kitchen so the reporter wouldn't have access to him. It was a tossup and the "big girl" part of me won.

"Off limits?" Cord asked as he settled into a chair in front of us.

I pursed my lips. "Considering our current purposes, let's

keep the topics current, and I'd prefer not to answer questions about Mr. Keller's previous sexual partners."

Joshua laughed and drank from his glass without saying a word.

Cord leaned forward and hit a few buttons on his keyboard. "How long have you and Joshua Keller been intimately involved?"

"Our personal relationship evolved from friendship into something more romantic in the last few weeks." It wasn't a lie exactly and it gave enough room for people to speculate that perhaps we were already a couple when the video came out. I glanced toward Joshua and he just smiled.

"Is the video of Mr. Keller leaving a popular BDSM club in the city a fake?"

"No."

"Does it upset you?"

Interesting question. "Not at all. The footage is nearly a year old. It's in his past and none of my business."

"You have to admit that it's caused some people to question his morals."

Joshua stiffened beside me and I took a sip of wine while I considered what to say. I knew Cord was phrasing his questions carefully and that he could have asked something so much more harsh and even cruel.

"I believe that what happens between consenting adults is their business and that if people disagree with that, I would encourage them to consider how they would feel if their sex life was exposed for public discussion and dissection. Not many would hold up under such scrutiny."

"His ex-girlfriend has accused you of ending their engagement."

"They were never engaged." I put one hand on Joshua's leg to keep him in place because I figured he was pretty close to jumping up. "And it's not really my problem if she wasn't woman enough to keep a man."

Cord's mouth dropped open and Joshua laughed, then relaxed against me.

"Huh." Cord leaned forward. "And her insinuation that you're somehow involved in the BDSM scene?"

"I've never been in the Playground or any other establishment of its kind. Since Ms. Carson cannot say the same, it would be in her best interests to keep her mouth shut."

Joshua drank from his glass, emptying it in one gulp, and set it aside. "Love."

"What?"

He just laughed. "Nothing. Please, Cord, do continue."

"So you don't participate in . . ." Cord flushed. "I mean . . ."

"Do I look like the kind of woman who would tolerate a man treating me with disrespect?" I asked softly. "Have you ever known me to let a man walk all over me?"

"No, and most definitely no."

"Then you can be assured that I demand respect in every arena in my life without exception." It was without a doubt the biggest nonanswer I'd ever given in my life, but he smiled and sat back in the chair.

"Mr. Keller, if I may, this recent scandal has put a spotlight on your private life that must be uncomfortable. Up until this point all of your statements have come from your PR firm. Is there anything you'd like to say about the situation last year?"

"The twins?"

"Yes, of course, the twins." Cord grinned when he said "twins" is if it were some magic word.

"I never discuss my relationships with women; not with friends and not with the press. It's unfortunate that they've chosen to be so indiscreet about the evening we spent together. At the time, I was a single man and I know very few men who'd pass up a chance to be with two beautiful women." Joshua's hand covered mine and used his thumb to rub my knuckles. The soft strokes were intoxicating in their gentleness and such a contrast to the hard, strong man that I knew him to be. "But what I will say is that I've found exactly what I'm looking for, and the press of this city will just have to find another man to trot along after looking for dirt."

Cord's gaze darted between us and drifted over our hands. Then he leaned forward. "Is that an admittance that your relationship is moving toward something more permanent?"

"That's private." Joshua turned my hand over and threaded his fingers through mine.

"Understood." He checked his watch. "I have a few more questions and then I'll get out of your hair."

"Thank you."

I closed the door and locked it with a sigh. "We make a good team." Turning to face him, I tilted my head and met his gaze across the room. "Am I what you've been looking for?"

He came to me, cupped my face with both hands, and kissed my lips softly. "Every time I look at you I'm reminded of how empty my life was before I met you. I filled myself with every excess I could get away with for years—women, booze, parties—and then I met you. The moment I laid eyes on you, I knew I had work to do."

"Work?" I sighed when he brushed his lips over mine again and then across my jaw.

"I had to clean up, live well, keep my career on path—because otherwise I would never deserve a woman like you."

"And what kind of woman am I?"

Joshua pushed both hands into my hair and fisted them. "Beautiful, strong, ambitious, sexy, and mine."

He moved closer, pressing his big amazing body against me,

and for a few seconds I forgot to breathe. It was stupid to get this worked up over a man basically claiming ownership but I couldn't even bring myself to deny it. I *was* his. I'd been his since the second he'd put his very talented hands on me.

"Is this the part where I beg for your cock?"

He laughed softly. "Sounds like a plan. Shall we discuss all the details or would you like to be surprised?"

"I love surprises." And no matter how crazy it was, I loved him, too.

Man in Motion

1

"Shhh, it's okay." The voice was like the richest cream, pouring over my mind, making the day bleed away; I closed my eyes in relief and relaxed in familiar arms. Having someone grab me from behind as I entered my apartment hadn't been on my agenda at all.

Was it Tuesday? No, of course not, but he was back early and that was a lovely little miracle. I sucked in a breath as large hands slid up my back and soft lips brushed down my neck. "Keep your eyes closed, Sonya, I want to play a game."

I really didn't need a present, not with him pressed against my back, his cock hard and thick against my ass. Caleb Howard was technically Kristen's client in the PR firm that I worked for. It was the only way I could really allow myself to indulge in the pure decadence of our affair. I didn't fool myself; he wasn't the sort of man who would settle down and marry me. Strictly speaking, I wasn't even all that sure I ever wanted to get married.

Something slinky and very cool slid down over my eyes and I laughed a little. A silk blindfold. That always meant something utterly delicious was about to happen to me. Caleb had never failed me in this regard; had never once left me wanting.

He prodded me through the doorway and into my apartment. I let my keys and purse drop on the floor as his body heat drifted away. I listened as he locked the door and engaged the security system. Did he want me to remain silent? I could do that. In fact, the idea of saying nothing while he stripped me down and fucked me absolutely stupid had so much appeal that lust rushed down my back fast and hard.

My nipples beaded against the material of my bra as fingers trailed down my arm. I shuddered a little and sighed when a firm hand settled at the small of my back to guide me. We went down the hallway and into what I knew was the bedroom. Good. I was in no mood to play, certainly not with the day I'd had.

"Is this okay, Sonya?" Lips brushed over mine and I nodded. "Good." He chuckled. "Very good."

I let him undress me, his large hands drifting over my body without a single hesitation. One of the best things about Caleb was his confidence, his ability to take control of a situation and in turn me. I trusted him. I trusted him to play little games like this with sex. I shuddered a little as cool air brushed against my now-naked back.

"Hard day?"

"Yes." I swallowed hard and gasped when blunt fingertips drifted over my nipples. "Very."

"Joshua Keller is a very bad boy." Caleb chuckled as he said it. "They looked hot in those pictures."

I couldn't help but laugh. "I can't discuss that."

"Oh, no need. That picture said *everything*." Caleb pulled my hair free and I wondered idly if I'd be able to find my hair-clip later. He had a habit of tossing them far and wide.

Hands slid through my hair and then down to my bare shoulders. His mouth brushed over mine and then he was gone. Seconds passed before he pressed an open-mouthed kiss against my stomach. "Wow."

"Just hold on, baby," Caleb murmured as his tongue dipped into my belly button.

I laughed as he removed my shoes and winced in dismay as they thudded across the room. The man had absolutely no respect for Jimmy Choo, but as he hooked his thumbs into my panties and pulled them down my legs I forgave him completely for the shoe treason he'd just committed.

"Jesus, woman."

"You like?" I asked as I remembered he hadn't seen me since I treated myself to a Saturday afternoon spa session with Tara that had included the most thorough waxing of my life. I loved the look and feel, but for the life of me I wasn't sure if I could ever consider that much pain a *relaxing* experience. It had jerked the Zen right out of my Chi, that was for certain.

"I love it." His lips brushed over my bare labia, then his tongue darted in and slid across my clit.

I squeaked, which was slightly embarrassing, and reached out to him to steady myself. Big hands slid up my legs, cupped my ass, and held me still for his questing tongue. My world narrowed, focusing on the talented mouth that explored my sex until I was shuddering and gasping—though I knew it was just the first of many orgasms to come.

Caleb lead me with careful hands to the bed and spread me out in the middle. His hands drifted down my legs to my ankles with casual familiarity. He spread my legs wide and I heard him take a deep breath. "I think you just gave me a new kink."

I laughed. He didn't needed any more. "Oops." He joined me on the bed after what seemed an unbearable amount of time and I shuddered as Caleb's strong, leanly muscled body slid over mine. "God."

"Not hardly, baby, but I make do." His mouth brushed over mine and I clutched at the bedspread beneath us. "I don't know how gentle this is going to be."

"I don't care." I gasped as he shoved his hands under my ass and filled me with his thick cock without another word. "Jesus."

"You're going to feel this for days."

I laughed and shuddered. "Promises, promises."

His body surged against mine, strong and heavy, and all I could do was cling to him and take each thrust of his cock with relief.

I woke up alone. After two years it wasn't even a surprise, but it still pissed me off. It was irritating that his early morning disappearing act still had the power to disappoint and anger me. I'd tried to rationalize it. After all, we had been together for two years and maybe I had a right to expect something from him after all this time. Together, in secret, for two years. That was my fault. I was the one who didn't want to fess up to fucking a client.

It had just been sex in the beginning. Wildly entertaining and satisfying sex that had both relaxed and soothed me. In the beginning, when the Marcus Group had still been in its infancy, I had spent too much time at work. A purely physical relationship served me best. Now I let myself fantasize about being with Caleb in public. I wondered how much flak he would get from people for being with a white woman and if it would bother him. Maybe it would bother him. Maybe that's why it was so easy for him to keep us a secret.

Disgruntled, I rolled out of bed and hauled my ass into the shower before I spent too much time wallowing in the situation I'd created. It was Saturday and I had a few things on my agenda for the day, including brunch with a potential new client. It was a relief to know that the lunch was still on. After the week we'd had with the Joshua Keller scandal, I'd half-expected Kevin Davis to cancel. Everyone knew the man to be devoutly religious and figured the naughty pictures of Tara and Joshua would have scared him off.

I grinned as I left the shower and started drying my hair. It was good to see Tara happy and very much in lust with a man. I figured she might love the man but she certainly wasn't admitting it currently. Tara had sacrificed a lot to get the Marcus Group off the ground, so it was nice to see her having some sort of social life even if she was getting tied down and spanked like a naughty, naughty girl in private.

I giggled at myself and sighed. I knew the situation had caused some tension at work. Kristen, the third person in our firm, was very prim and proper. I had no idea how she was really handling everything. I figured I'd find out soon enough, though; Kristen wasn't the kind to keep things to herself for any length of time.

By the time I had dressed and packed a lighter purse for the day, I'd nearly gotten over being pissed at Caleb. It wasn't his fault, no matter how much I'd prefer to lay it at his feet. I had made that naughty bed and it was my duty to sleep in it until I found a way how to fix things. It was high time that I figured out what I even wanted from him.

The trip from my apartment to the restaurant where I was meeting the new client took longer than I anticipated but I still arrived in plenty of time to get settled at the table and look through my notes. Kevin Davis was a second-round draft pick for the Atlanta Falcons. He'd finished college with a degree in business and came from a religious household. His parents were evangelicals but he'd separated himself from their church when he'd gone pro.

He arrived a few minutes late with a smooth apology that I felt was entirely fake but well delivered. For a twenty-five-year-old, he was surprisingly adept in social situations and managed to order food without making an ass out of himself. I figured that was an improvement from some of the clients we'd dealt with in the past. Thank God Atlanta didn't have a hockey team.

"My parents don't think I need a PR firm to represent me."

"What does your agent think?" I asked, skipping over the parents. It was never a good idea to actively conflict with clients' parents. Many of our clients were still young enough that the parents were often very strong influences.

"He made the appointment," Kevin admitted. "He says I need to work on my image so I don't look like some hick."

I pursed my lips and swallowed back distaste at his choice of words. "You present a nice, wholesome image to the public, Kevin, and that works in your favor. You have a few sponsors and a good endorsement deal. Those are all things we can work with."

He reached out and put his hand over mine. "Yeah, I'm looking forward to working with the Marcus Group." His thumb moved over the top of my wrist in a caress and a chill of genuine horror ran down my back. "Everyone says that you're all very dedicated and like to provide personalized service to your clients. That's what I'm looking for, Sonya, personalized service."

My mouth absolutely did not fall open . . . because my jaw was clenched so tight that I'd probably just paid for a semester of college tuition for my dentist's kid in under thirty seconds. I carefully extracted my hand from under his and sat back in the chair. "You know, I don't think you're a fit for the Marcus Group."

His eyes darkened and he smirked. "Is that so?"

"It is." I carefully picked up my Blackberry and dropped it into my purse. "I'll let your agent know that we are declining the offer to represent you."

"You know I'm popular in this town. People like me. Lots of people like me."

I stood and shook back my hair. "You're the flavor of the season, kid; next year there will be a new, faster, prettier version of you and you'll be lucky to play a single game."

He grabbed my arm as I passed him, his fingers wrapped around my wrist like a band of steel. "Sit down, Ms. Carson, we aren't finished with this discussion. You can't just dismiss me."

"Let me go before people start paying attention," I snapped under my breath and then tugged briefly. "Physically restraining a woman three times smaller than you isn't going to be good press, Mr. Davis."

Kevin smiled then, but his eyes remained dark and angry. "It certainly wouldn't look good for your little PR firm if you caused a scene in one of the city's most popular restaurants." His grip tightened. "Take a seat."

I leaned down so I could whisper in his ear. "You are too young and too stupid to realize what kind of mistake you are making. Neither your agent nor your coach would appreciate it if it got out that you liked to hurt women. In fact, in some circles in this area, behavior like this could get your ass kicked."

He jerked me closer and whispered back. "Are you a whore like your boss? I bet you'd look great sucking my cock."

"Let go." I winced as he released my wrist and I straightened away. "Don't ever contact me again."

"We have an agreement. Today was just a formality."

"The Marcus Group will not be representing you, Mr. Davis." On the way out of the restaurant I stopped and put his tab on our corporate account and set up a limit so he wouldn't buy a stupid amount of alcohol.

I didn't notice I was shaking until I was sitting in my car in the parking garage two blocks away. It was the last thing I'd expected and I felt foolish for not anticipating some sort of backlash. Tara and Joshua had a new relationship and the pictures that had come out were very intimate—not sex, but enough to put that idea into the heads of some people. I rubbed my wrist and sighed at the bruise that was already starting. Having to report what had happened to Tara was going to be difficult, and now on top of it the stupid bastard had bruised me.

Caleb was sprawled on my couch when I came home. I hadn't expected to see him again, so I was a little surprised and a little relieved. "Hey."

He looked me over and tossed the TV remote on the table. "What happened with you and Kevin Davis?"

I frowned at him. "Excuse me?"

"Look, I recommended the Marcus Group to the kid because I figured you guys would be good for him. God knows he needs all the help he can get and I told our coach I would help him out. I thought you'd reached an agreement and today was just a formality. He called and told me that you declined to represent him."

I stared for a long moment, my heart racing, my stomach clenching in some strange agony. "I see. Did you tell him about our 'personalized service'?"

He frowned. "I told him that you guys worked hard for all of your clients and that you were all career oriented. I explained how Kristen helped me get a plan together for endorsements and let me pick which ones suited me best." He stood up. "What the hell happened, Sonya?"

I took a deep breath. "You know I don't discuss business with you, Caleb." I tossed my purse aside. "We're not representing Davis and it would be in his best interests if you suggested he seek out a male PR agent." I walked into the kitchen, dug out a bottle of wine, and poured myself a glass without another word.

Half the glass was gone by the time he came into the kitchen after me. "He made a pass at you."

"I'm not discussing it." My grip tightened on the wineglass and I looked away from him just as the doorbell rang. It was my luck. "Stay here."

"I'm not hiding in the kitchen," he snapped. "I'm pretty damn tired of hiding all together, to be honest."

"Yeah, well, maybe if you didn't disappear with the rising sun we could discuss having a public relationship." I glared at him over my shoulder so that he would stay in the kitchen and stalked to my door. Throwing it open without checking to see who was there was probably a mistake but that's neither here nor there. "Kevin, what the hell are you doing here?"

He shoved at the door and I stumbled back a little. "We need to have a private conversation. I told you I wasn't going to be dismissed, Sonya."

"You are an idiot."

He reached out, grabbed my arm, and jerked me toward him. "And you're a cock tease."

"Let her go."

Davis released my arm immediately. "Hey, Caleb, didn't realize you were here."

"I can see that." Caleb walked to stand beside me. "What the fuck is going on here?"

Davis flushed, his eyes hard. "I didn't realize she was your piece, Howard."

I really didn't expect to Caleb to hit him, but then neither did Kevin . . . which was why he ended up sprawled in the hallway in front of my door, right at Tara Marcus's feet. "Shit."

Tara looked from Kevin Davis to Caleb to me and then sighed. "Shit, indeed." She pulled out her phone and dialed. "Joshua, you should park the car. I think I'm going to be here a while."

I winced at her tone and finished off my wine in a long swallow.

Tara nudged Kevin with her foot. "Get up and go home. I told you that I would speak with you on Monday."

"Fine." He rolled to his feet, shot Caleb a dark, angry look, and left.

I needed more wine. Well, I needed a long bath, a massage, a bottle of wine, and maybe a few orgasms. Two or three; I'm not a greedy girl. In the kitchen, I retrieved another glass and poured Tara some as well. It was too damn early in the day to be drinking but I figured she wouldn't be in much better shape than me after I finished answering her questions.

She dropped her purse on the kitchen counter and took the wineglass with a small smile. "So."

"Yeah."

"How long?"

It wasn't the question I'd anticipated. I figured she'd immediately want to know what had happened with Kevin. I flushed. "A while."

"Huh." She took a sip of wine and leaned against the counter across from me. "Kevin called and told me you left lunch abruptly. He implied that you were rude and combative."

"That about sums up my part," I admitted softly. With a sigh, I set aside my wine and crossed my arms. "It's not good, Tara."

"Well, I figured it wasn't going to be. He's a big client and you were quite proud of the acquisition." Her gaze dropped to my hands. "How did you get that bruise?"

"He didn't want me to leave so he tried to force me to sit back down at the table." I moved away from the counter so I wouldn't pick up the wine again. It was too tempting and the last thing I wanted was to develop the habit of drowning my anger or my sorrow in the bottom of a bottle.

"So, just say it."

I laughed. "Just say it?"

"Yeah."

"He implied that sex came with the contract, called you a whore, and said I would look great sucking his cock." It all rushed out of my mouth and I slumped down into a chair when I was finished. Who knew the truth would be so exhausting? "Then he shows up here, calls me a cock tease and a piece of ass . . ."

"And Caleb Howard punched him in the face," Tara pressed her lips together in a thin line. "Fuck."

"Yep." I gave up fighting it and went back to get my glass of wine. "He called to complain to you, huh?"

"I guess he figured that I would take his side." Tara was staring into her wineglass, her mouth drawn into a tight line of misery. "I'm sorry he turned out to be an asshole."

"Do not apologize to me."

"I knew that we'd catch some flak for the pictures. I mean, everyone in the whole damn country has seen them and they look so . . ."

"Intimate." I supplied the word because I figured she might say something mean and I didn't want that for her. "Tara, that moment was private and someone took a picture of it and gave it to the world. That doesn't take away from what it was and I'm just really sorry this happened to you."

She nodded. "It could have been so much worse."

"Yeah, he could have managed to get your panties off." I wiggled my eyebrows and she grinned, very reluctantly.

"We're . . ." She sighed. "I should call Kristen and talk to her. We both know that this might not be an isolated incident."

"For the time being I think we should only agree to meet clients in the office, where we'll have each other as backup." I shrugged when she looked my way. "Look, you and I can handle ourselves in a public situation. I don't know what Kristen would have done or how she would have reacted if it had been her today instead of me."

"We can't isolate her from it."

"But we can minimize the public fallout."

"Granted." Tara finished off her wine and eyed the bottle. "Shit." She sat the glass aside, corked the bottle, and put it back in my wine fridge. "You know drinking is not the road to take."

I nodded and stared at what was left in my glass. "Yeah. It's just easy."

"Too easy," she cautioned.

A blush tore across my face and I put the glass down. "Okay, so . . ."

"I'll contact Davis's agent and let him know that we aren't

interested and that he should tighten the leash on his client if he doesn't want a serious press problem." She eyed my wrist. "Unless you'd like to press charges."

I shook my head. "No, that's the last thing we need. It doesn't even hurt that much. You know I bruise easily."

"He had no business putting his hands on you." She crossed her arms. "We could weather the publicity and he deserves some backlash on this."

"I'm sure the black eye he's going to be sporting for the next week will make up for it and I don't think he's stupid enough to tell anyone how he got it." I glanced toward the door she had closed and sighed. "I wonder what those two are out there discussing?"

"God knows." She grimaced. "I'd rather Joshua not know what Davis said about me; he'll just get all bent out of shape."

"Yeah, I can see that."

Joshua and Caleb weren't in the living room. In fact, they weren't in the apartment at all. Tara sighed and dropped down on the couch. "That's just fucking great. You know they went . . ." The door opened then and Caleb strolled in with Joshua trailing along behind him, a little smile on his face. "What did *you* do?"

"Nothing" was the dual response and they looked about as innocent as a forty-year-old hooker which was to say not at all.

"Oh, come on. If you hit him again you know he'll . . ." I sucked in a breath. "What did you do, Caleb?"

"I didn't lay a finger on the kid. We have a game next week." Caleb dropped down in the chair. "The coach would skin me alive if he couldn't play." He grinned as Joshua slid onto the couch beside Tara. "It was inspired, though."

Joshua laughed. "Yeah, it was."

"Is this going to involve the police?" Tara asked as she rubbed her face with both hands.

"No. I don't think he'll be reporting it to the police." Joshua plucked up one of her hands and rubbed it carefully between his. "What's he going to say? That he got so freaked out by two men just staring at him that he pissed his pants?"

"You just stared?"

"Well, we were having a conversation . . . with each other . . . in his vicinity." Caleb stretched. "About castration."

"Castra—?" I demanded.

"Yeah, you know I was pre-vet in college. I figure after I finish with football I might go to vet school." He smiled. "I used to work in a vet's office, ya know."

"Really." I sighed. "He pissed his pants?"

Tara started laughing. It was a rich, warm sound that did more to relax me than the two nearly full glasses of wine I'd had since I got home. She buried her face against the side of Joshua's neck and giggled softly for nearly two minutes before she got control of herself. She relaxed against him and sighed.

Finally, she lifted her head. "We're going to be late for lunch with my father."

Joshua stood and offered her his hand. "I'm telling him that you're to blame for the pictures."

She eyed him. "I would expect no less from you." She took his hand and stood. "I'll call Kristen later tonight and tell her what happened. We'll need to work on a few plans to . . . smooth this little problem out."

"Agreed."

I followed them to the door, took the quick hug for the physical reassurance it was, and locked the door carefully. "So."

"Not so much a secret anymore," Caleb murmured.

"Two years with no one knowing and we manage to out ourselves to three different people in ten minutes." I turned and stared at him. "And I'll have to face the Spanish Inquisition on Monday from the two of them."

"I'm sure that Davis will manage to tell the whole team."

Caleb stood and rubbed his head. "So, I've got to attend this charity thing tonight. I'd planned on going alone because . . . well, CeCe told me she was tired of being my pretend girlfriend in public."

I laughed. "She was good to do it at all."

"Apparently, she's got some guy at work she's really interested in who she can't pursue because of me." Caleb sighed. "I felt like an asshole when she told me. It never really crossed my mind that I was fucking with her life that way."

"She should have said something sooner." I had a feeling that CeCe Richards, Caleb's longtime friend, had been using him as an excuse to avoid men but I wasn't going to say that aloud. He wore guilt well and maybe she'd get a gift or two out of him for her trouble. "Is this your half-assed way of asking me to go with you?"

"Yes."

"Are you sure?" I frowned. "I mean, won't you get flak for . . ." I flushed. "I mean, I'm white."

He laughed. "Yeah, I noticed."

"You know what I mean." I crossed my arms. "You've only ever dated black women."

"You aren't the first white woman I've ever dated. I was with a girl in college for almost two years. . . ." He trailed off. "At any rate, I don't care what anyone says about that. Color is . . . what it is. What about you? How do you feel about being seen in public with a black man?"

I frowned at him. "You know I don't give a shit about any of that crap."

"Then this discussion is pointless. Do you want to go to the charity thing with me or not?"

"How formal?"

"Dinner party."

"Okay." I nodded before I could think of a logical reason to tell him no. "We can do that. What time will you pick me up?"

2

The entire time I was getting ready, I tried to talk myself out of going. It was stupid. I shouldn't even be interested in going out with him in public, not when I knew he wasn't going to give up his after-sex disappearing act. For the first year, it hadn't bothered me. In fact, I'd been kind of relieved to wake up alone. But gradually it had started to hurt and that had made me feel stupid, which in turn had pissed me off.

I hadn't had a serious relationship since college. In fact, for a very long time, I'd made a point of avoiding men who wanted anything permanent or serious. The casual sex relationship I'd been exploring with Caleb Howard for two years had been all that I needed—except lately I'd started to want more and that made no sense. The man wasn't going to settle down with me and really, did I even want that?

He was a grown-up child, really. He liked fast cars, liked to party, and prided himself on never letting a woman tie him down. But he did other things, too, things that were hard to ignore. He volunteered at youth centers, attended charity events for the Humane Society, and had started a program for the city

103

to educate people and combat animal cruelty. Caleb was far more than the sum of his parts and that made it difficult to dismiss him.

He was also, much to my dismay, utterly beautiful. The first time I'd seen him my mouth had dropped open and I'd been gasping for air ever since. Caleb Howard was six feet of sleekly sculpted muscle and power. He moved in a graceful economy of motion on and off the field that caught and kept attention. Most athletes were courted by Nike and other sports equipment companies. Caleb had appeared in *Calvin Klein* ads and graced the cover of *GQ* in the best Armani could put out.

"Having fun?"

I offered him a smile and let him lead me toward a table where a good portion of the offensive line for the Atlanta Falcons were lounging about. Thankfully, their rookie quarterback seemed to be missing. I really wasn't up to dealing with Kevin Davis again anytime soon. I knew most of the other men—who were, in fact, clients of mine. One was married, so I met a wife and then a variety of girlfriends I'd probably never see again.

Caleb was prodding me toward a chair when I heard my name being called. I turned and relaxed a little. "Mr. Marcus."

Andrew Marcus, Tara's globe-trotting father, offered me a smile and pulled me in for a hug. "I've told you that you can call me Andrew."

I really couldn't. The man had grounded me once when we were fifteen and I spent the summer with Tara in their house in the Caymans. I'd have better luck calling him Daddy, which made me blush a little as stupid as that was. "You know Caleb Howard?"

Caleb offered his hand. "Sir."

"Yes, Caleb has done great work for Youth Challenge." Andrew shook his hand with a warm smile and then refocused on me. "I saw Tara for lunch. She seemed out of sorts."

"We had a bit of a day."

"Yes." He nodded. "So it appeared." He brushed his fingers gently over my cheek. "You'll let me know if I can do anything to make things easier. She doesn't let me help her the way she should."

"Success is more satisfying when you earn it."

Andrew laughed. "I much preferred it when you girls were plotting some unfortunate boy's downfall and practicing cheers in my backyard. I'm rather concerned that I let the lot of you loose on my favorite city." He nodded to Caleb. "Nice to see you, Caleb. Watch out for this one; she's rotten just like my Tara."

"Well, beautiful women are meant to be spoiled, sir." Caleb settled in my chair as Andrew Marcus walked away. "You were a cheerleader?"

"Yeah, high school and college."

He sat down beside me and grinned. "Please tell me you still have the uniforms."

"You're a freak," I declared and everyone at the table started laughing. "Of course, I do."

Caleb grinned when several of the men groaned. "Awesome."

The meal passed in a blur but I'd done enough of those kinds of parties in the past that it was easy to participate in the conversation without revealing a whole lot. Besides, most of the conversation was about football. I knew football. I represented ten of Caleb's fellow players. I reached out for my water glass and the bracelet I'd been using to cover up the bruise on my wrist slid down my arm. I snatched it back but one of the women across the table had seen it. She was a *wife* and there was really nothing like a pro–football player's wife. They were strong willed, often hot-tempered creatures who enjoyed the money and the fame, and if they were smart they watched their husbands like hawks. Susan Willis was for all intents and purposes the "team wife." She expected her husband to toe the line and all the men around him had to toe it, too.

"That looks painful." She glanced toward Caleb, her gaze decidedly icy.

"Not so much." I met her gaze and then smiled. "I'm the palest woman on earth and I bruise easily." She started to speak and I inclined my head. "Of course not. The man donates money to children's charities and fosters puppies, for fuck's sake."

She sighed. "Sorry, Caleb."

He shrugged it off. "She had a disagreement with someone." He smiled then. "If it helps, I punched him in the face."

"It helps," Susan assured him. She smiled then. "You aren't the palest woman on earth." She jerked her head. "Delilah Wallace-Rainey over there in the red has you beat by a country mile. She is most assuredly the whitest woman I've ever seen."

I bit down on my lip. "I sort of always considered her more transparent than white. If you get too close you can see her blood moving."

Susan grinned. "Yeah, it's rather revolting."

"She's old money." I ran my finger around the top of my glass. "It makes her a dangerous enemy, an interesting friend, and a wretched gossip. Have you met her?"

"Not formally."

I chuckled. "Would you like to? You're heading up the committee for the holiday food drive this year, right? We could probably talk her out of money. She loves to give money away; it makes her feel superior."

Susan nodded. "I'm always game to take someone else's money."

I stood and slid away from the table. "Be warned, she *air* kisses and she'll probably ask you if you know any famous black people besides the one you're married to." I raised an eyebrow.

She laughed. "Wow, let's see . . . I met Michelle Obama last summer. Do you think that will count?"

"Not as much as Will Smith but it should do in a pinch."

"So, did I pass the test?"

Caleb frowned as he put the car into DRIVE. "What test?"

"Come on . . ."

He laughed. "Susan liked you and that fat check you got for her food drive thing. You know that's her baby."

"Yeah, I got roped into doing PR for it while we were in the ladies' room." I wasn't upset about it. It was a good cause and I could have easily deflected her if I hadn't wanted to be involved.

"No test, though. It was nice being out with someone I actually . . ." He sighed. "It was just nice not having to pretend. CeCe liked these parties because she liked meeting people but we're just friends and I think people who know me were starting to catch on."

"No one brought her up." Which had been a surprise. I'd really figured I would be grilled within an inch of my life when I'd been crowded into the ladies' room with the rest of the women from the table. But I hadn't. Susan had asked one or two pointed questions about the bruise on my wrist and I'd assured her again that Caleb hadn't done it.

"You thought they might bring her up?"

"Yeah."

"I don't think Susan liked CeCe, to be honest." Caleb shrugged as he pulled into my apartment building's underground garage. "It was just . . . they didn't mesh. CeCe was too much of a party girl for Susan's peace of mind. But, you're a career woman and she digs women who get their own. You know, she's a lawyer."

"I did know. I make it my business to know such things." I unbuckled my seat belt. "You coming up?"

He paused and then shook his head. "No, I've got a game." He leaned in and kissed my mouth. "You know, why don't you come tomorrow? You could sit in the team skybox. Susan and a few of the other wives will be up there playing hostess and feeding everyone."

"Do you want me to go?"

"Well, yeah, I do."

"Leave me a ticket at the box office, then."

"Cool." He kissed me again and then sighed. "I'd really like to come up but . . ."

"No sex the night before the game?" I grinned. "It could be bad luck if you broke your rule."

"Yeah." He frowned. "I have stupid rules."

I licked my lips. "Just think how great it will be tomorrow. You're always bouncing off the walls after a game." I leaned in and rubbed my lips over his. "We'll come back to my apartment and fuck for hours."

"You're evil," he groaned. "I'll walk you up and make sure you don't have any uninvited guests."

I had my hair in big, fat rollers the next morning when I opened the door for Kristen and Tara. They'd called in advance so the beauty of their arrival was that they'd come with breakfast and much-needed coffee. "I have two hours."

"How is your wrist?" Tara asked.

I showed her and grimaced at the dark brown bruise that still circled it. "It's fine, really. Stop worrying about it."

"You made the society column this morning." Kristen dropped the paper on the table as Tara unpacked breakfast. "Lots of buzz on the disappearance of the old girlfriend and you looking all hot in a black dress."

"Are you upset that I'm dating him?"

"No. I'm upset that you hid it," Kristen admitted. "I

thought we were friends, and from the looks of things you've been hiding this for a while."

"You guys are my best friends." And I really didn't want to admit to them that I'd had a mostly meaningless sexual affair with a man who had never once bothered to stick around until morning. It made me feel . . . dirty, and I didn't like that feeling at all. "It was a mutual decision, and really, there isn't much to talk about. It's sex. Last night was the first time we've ever even gone somewhere in public together. I don't know that we'd have done it if we hadn't basically been outed by Kevin Davis already. God knows he's probably spreading some story far and wide about us. We both figured if we appeared in public on a date that it would take the wind out of his sails."

"Does anyone know about the argument or the fight?"

"Not that I'm aware of. It hasn't hit any news services and I think he'll keep his mouth shut about it. His agent will surely make sure he doesn't look like an asshole." I broke a scone in half and shrugged. "I mean, I don't think he's going to admit to what provoked Caleb into hitting him and Caleb isn't known for that kind of bad behavior. Everyone will assume that Davis did something to provoke him."

"Agreed." Kristen relaxed in her chair. "So, just sex, huh? I knew that he wasn't really dating CeCe. I was beginning to think she was his beard."

I sputtered and choked on the coffee I barely managed to swallow. "Wow."

She laughed. "Well, he had a fake girlfriend. Most guys have a fake girlfriend so they can pretend to be straight or to, you know, avoid their matchmaking mother. Since he never took the fake girlfriend home to Chicago to meet his mother I had to assume it wasn't for her."

"Yeah, he's so not gay." I grinned then. "But it would be kind of hot to watch him kiss another guy."

Tara and Kristen both laughed.

"He did this photo shoot for Eddie Bauer." Kristen blushed. "All of those beautiful models and him. They were all giddy and asking for his autograph. I think practically everyone in the room—male and female—would have slept with him given a chance."

I finished off a scone and sat back in my chair with my coffee. "He never spends the night." I bit down on my lip. That was not what I'd meant to say. I averted my gaze and sighed. "Ever."

"Well, have you ever asked?"

I grimaced at Tara's question and shrugged. "Should I have to ask? I mean, he would stay if he wanted to and obviously he doesn't want to. It's like he's always moving. Then he goes and does what he did yesterday. I told him to stay in the kitchen."

"So, how long?" Kristen asked again.

"Two years." I blushed as I said it. "Not so serious or frequent at first. I mean, I really didn't even think there would be a second time. But he kept showing up and we kept going to bed. The sex is fantastic but we've never had much more than that. The last six months it's been a weekly thing but he's always gone before I wake up."

"So last night was really the first time you ever even went out in public together?" Kristen asked. When I looked at her she was frowning. "Seriously?"

"It was sex. Just sex."

"And now it's not."

"Now . . . I don't know what the hell it is." I closed my eyes. "Now it's dinner parties and sitting in the team skybox with a bunch of girlfriends and wives. Now it's . . . being in the society column and looking like he's serious about me but what if it's still just sex for him? What if *I* really don't want it to be more than sex?" I hated even saying it aloud. I hated myself for the question and the weakness it represented. "I'm screwed."

"So, huh." Tara took a deep breath. "Look, there is a lot of history between the two of you and wow; I can't believe the two of you kept this a secret for two freaking years. I knew there was something going on for a while and I figured it was a client . . . but not him."

I snorted. "Like I want to admit to anyone that I'm letting a man use me for sex."

"You're using him for sex as much as he's using you," Kristen put in. "It cuts both ways, Sonya."

"Yeah."

The skybox wasn't overly crowded but upon entering I wished I'd dragged Tara or Kristen along with me, which made me feel really foolish. I was a grown woman and I could surely handle hanging out with a bunch of people I didn't know to watch my . . . boyfriend play a little football. Jesus, was he my boyfriend? It had taken me six months to call him my lover instead of my fuck buddy and now . . . shit. Now he was my *boyfriend* in my foolish little head.

"Hey."

I glanced at Susan Willis as I dug a Diet Coke out of a cooler. "Hi. Did you need help with anything?"

"No, we're good. Kickoff is in a few minutes. I saved you a seat beside me up front." She motioned. "Caleb told Tom you'd probably come today. He was excited to have you here."

I raised an eyebrow. "He's never really seemed to care if I even watch his games."

"They try to act like they don't care but they do."

I followed her down a few stairs to the seats and pulled off the jacket. "It took me forever to find a team T-shirt this morning. I probably have like twenty that don't fit." I waved my hand out over the field. "I have ten clients on the team; they all bring me shirts." I grinned then. "As small as possible, of course. The guys are kind of transparent."

She laughed. "I bet." She was silent for a moment and then sighed. "So, Kevin Davis hurt you yesterday."

I choked on my drink and swallowed painfully. "What?"

"It was kind of hard to miss his black eye this morning. The coach had both of them in the office for twenty minutes. Tom seemed really upset as well but they aren't talking about it." She raised an eyebrow.

"I can't talk about it." I looked out over the bright green field with a frown. "It was business and I can't talk about it."

"Okay, I get that. Just let me know if you need anything on that front. I handle harassment cases all the time, and if he doesn't get his head on straight, I'm not afraid to slap a few pieces of paper on his narrow little arrogant ass."

I chuckled. "Good to know."

I made it halfway through the game before I lost my cool, jumped to my feet, and yelled at a referee who had no hope whatsoever of hearing me. I blushed when I realized that half the people in the box were staring at me in shock. The other half were grinning. I sat down, disgruntled. "What?"

Susan laughed. "Nothing, girl; you go right ahead and tell him how you feel."

"It was a bad call! A blind man would have made a better decision." I slouched down in my seat and a man behind me patted me on the shoulder. I glanced back at him and grinned when he winked.

After the third quarter I went in search of a sandwich and another drink. I'd noticed that Susan had pretty much kept herself glued to my side since I arrived but she let me wander off for food without her. I'd fixed a small plate and grabbed a few extra cookies when I noticed that I was no longer alone at the counter. I offered the woman a sideways look when I realized she was leaning and staring.

"Hey."

She frowned. "I didn't realize that Caleb and CeCe had broken up."

I sighed. "I really don't know much about that. You'll have to ask him." I sure as hell wasn't going to say anything that I did know. I wasn't exactly sure how well it would go over.

"I also didn't realize that he went for skinny little white girls."

Great. "Well, there is no accounting for taste." I offered her a bright smile and grabbed another cookie. "You should ask him about that, too. I'm sure he'd *love* to have that conversation with you."

I walked back to the seats and dropped down beside Susan. Who glanced my way as she stole a cookie from my plate. "You look . . ." She turned and looked around the skybox with an irritated sigh. "What?"

"Apparently, I'm a skinny white girl."

Susan snorted and then turned to look at me in horror. "Wait . . . you're white?"

I laughed. "Jerk."

She grinned and bit into the cookie. "Man, you white girls are sneaky wenches. Never know when one is just going to show up."

I managed to get out of the after-game party by pleading a headache. It wasn't that I didn't like Susan; in fact, I liked her a lot. She was smart, funny, and really just one of those great people. I just didn't want to hang out with a bunch of girlfriends and wives and pretend that I was one of them. I wasn't Caleb's girlfriend. I wasn't sure I wanted to be his girlfriend. I was his *piece* and I really had to remember that.

He showed up five hours after the game, leaning in my doorway all sexy and relaxed like he owned the world. He always looked like that after he won a game; it was almost as attractive as his brooding, sort of pissed-off face when they lost. The sex was meaner when the team lost. Either way I had a great time. But, I wasn't foolish enough to say that aloud. Men, especially professional athletes, had a thing about luck and women talking about games being "lost."

"Still have a headache?"

I motioned him in and shut the door. "It's mostly gone."

"Susan said you got some flak from Rachel James."

"Is that her name?" I shrugged. Her husband wasn't one of my clients and I didn't know all of the "wives" on the team by sight. "She called me a skinny little white girl and wanted to know when you and CeCe broke up. I brushed her off and it wasn't a big deal."

"Then why didn't you go to the after party?"

I turned on him and glared. "Look, Caleb, we fuck. We fuck regularly. I'm not the woman you want on your arm in public; you made that abundantly clear over the past two years. If CeCe hadn't decided she was 'done' playing your girlfriend for the press you never would have taken me to that dinner last night. I don't know why you wanted me at the game today . . . maybe because you thought Susan expected it?"

" 'We fuck,' " he repeated, his voice low with anger.

"That's right. We fuck." I crossed my arms and glared at him. "I happen to like that part a lot but I'm not going to run around pretending this thing between us is more than that when it clearly isn't." I jerked my T-shirt over my head and walked toward the bedroom. "Now, you can come to bed and fuck me or you can go home. It's up to you."

I didn't expect him to follow me but he was on me before I even reached the bed. His big hands were firm but gentle as he took over undressing me. I barely had time to register what he had planned before I was sprawled out in the middle of my bed and he was on top of me.

He pinned both of my arms to the bed above my head and glared down at me. "We fuck."

"Yeah. We *fuck*." I struggled against him and shuddered a little at the way his clothes rubbed against my skin.

"If that's what you want me from, Sonya, that's what you'll get." He lifted away and used one hand to unzip his jeans. His fingers tightened around my wrists as he worked his cock out of his boxers.

"Jesus."

It was depraved how turned on I was but I couldn't help myself. I watched him work the dark, swollen flesh of his cock for several seconds before he moved upward, shoved himself between my thighs, and pressed right into me.

"So wet," he murmured and then laughed harshly. "You're such a little freak."

"Yes." I arched up off the bed and put my feet flat on the bed. "Fuck."

Each stroke was hard, relentless, and just painful enough to make my whole body hum with relief. He fisted his free hand in my hair as he powered into me, his breath ragged against my throat. It was almost mean and absolutely delicious. I loved every second of it. The hot glide of his flesh into mine, the barely re-strained violence of his clothed body, and hard little groans that he tried to swallow but couldn't were enough to make me wish I made him mad every single time we had sex.

He yanked on my hair, slammed into me, and demanded in a low, hard voice, "Come. Come right now."

I shuddered and fought it against him. Giving into him seemed unreasonable and wrong in that moment but he thrust into me again and I shattered with a sob. My body bowed up against his and I came in a rush of wetness against his invading cock. He groaned and his whole body jerked as he came, too.

Caleb was still on me for several seconds and then he lifted off of me. He slid off the bed and stood in front of me for a long minute, his dark gaze confused and still angry. With shaking hands he put himself away, zipped his jeans, and left without a word. I dropped back on my bed and tried not to flinch when I heard the front door of apartment shut with a little bang.

"Damn it." I rolled off the bed and went into the bathroom.

I avoided the mirror completely. The last thing I wanted to see was my own face, not after what I had just done. Under the spray of too-hot water, I let myself break a little but not enough to actually cry. I hadn't cried over a man since my junior year of college and I sure as hell wasn't going to start now.

It was difficult to admit, even to myself, but having him leave immediately after sex without a word was so much worse than him waiting until I was asleep. It didn't help that I'd done it to myself.

3

Work on Monday proved to be an exercise in martyrdom. Tara was still trying to figure out what Jean Turst, the reporter who had leaked the pictures of Tara and Joshua, wanted from us and the woman had so far dodged several meetings with Tara. Kristen was nervous and on edge. She'd been that way since the whole thing with Joshua and the video had started. It was almost like she had a secret of her own just waiting to be exposed. They were both a little wounded over my little secret, and as much as I regretted hurting them, I couldn't feel bad for keeping it to myself.

Sex is private. Sex should be just about the most private thing that happens between two people and I still wasn't interested in talking about it. Especially now that I'd ruined a relationship that had been built on respect and pleasure. Now what I had with Caleb was something mean and a little harder than I'd thought he was capable of.

Tara let me stew most of the day behind my computer and four monitors before she propped one hip on my desk, crossed her arms, and stared. "So."

"So?" I asked with a raised eyebrow.

"You go on a date, take in a football game, and come in on Monday looking like someone ran over your cat and stopped to brag about it."

"I don't have a cat."

"Maybe you should get one. I understand they are good for stress relief."

Great. I'd get a cat. Then I'd get another cat to keep the first cat company when I was at work. I'd be an old cat lady inside a year. It was horrifying to even think about. I slumped down in my chair. "I don't want a stupid cat."

"Most cats are fairly intelligent. How about one of those silly little dogs you could buy clothes for?" She grinned as she said it. "Or, you know, you could grow some balls, start figuring out how to stop Caleb Howard from running around in your life like he's in charge, and tell the man what you really want from him."

I crossed my arms. "He's just a man. A sex toy with two legs and a job. I can get another one just like him in a day."

"Sure. Sure. He must not know about you," Tara said airily and walked away with a little laugh.

I hated her a little but I found myself laughing anyway. There was nothing I could really say to that. I was being a great big twit about Caleb and we all knew it. The truth was that I didn't even know why I was being so horrible about it and self-analysis had never really been a hobby of mine.

He was in lounging on my couch when I came home. I frowned at him and dropped my computer bag by a chair. "Huh."

Caleb turned off the television and tossed the remote aside. "So, here's the thing. You copped a serious attitude with me and I responded in a way that I'm not proud of. I've never treated a woman like that in my life and I don't even know why I'm here because I've been fucking pissed at you all day."

I bit down on my bottom lip to keep from laughing. "Still mad at me?"

"Yes!" He pointed a finger at me. "You acted like an asshole and I in turned acted like . . . I did not act like the man my mother raised, that's for certain. It's stupid to blame you because I'm responsible for my own actions. Now I'm just pissed and irritated over the whole fucking thing and I . . . look, woman . . ."

My mouth dropped open. "Woman?"

He left the couch and walked to a window to stare out of it. "You said when I first talked you into bed that it was just sex. I figured I could deal with that because I wanted you and getting a little of you was better than getting nothing."

Wow. *That* was not what I expected him to say.

"CeCe says you have commitment issues." He turned and stared at me. "Am I going to be reduced to watching old episodes of Oprah and Dr. Phil until I can figure out the rules with you? Because right now I'm not even sure what game you're playing but I feel like I've been penalized for wanting more of you. I've always wanted more, and yes, I did act a little impulsively on Saturday. I know I sprang that on you and you were already off balance because of what had happened at lunch."

"You can't just decide you want *more*! That is . . . that is a mutual decision."

"Yeah, well, outside of the bedroom, you have the communication skills of a rock—unless you are at work—so how the fuck am I supposed to know what you want?" He crossed his arms, and if he weren't a grown man I would've sworn he was pouting.

"A rock? Look, Caleb, we've had a good thing going for a long time and you were the one who changed the rules. How the hell am I supposed to know you want more when you don't even bother to stay the whole night?"

He stared at me, the muscle in his jaw jumping. "That's the second time you've said that. What's the last thing you say to me before you go to sleep, Sonya?"

"What?"

"What is the last thing you say to me before you go to sleep?" He repeated it very slowly and I tried not to glare at him for the patronizing tone.

I frowned and then took a deep breath. "I tell you to make sure you lock the door when you leave."

"You've said that to me every single time I've ever been in your bed. Even the first night. It is obvious to me that you want—or at the very least expect—me to leave."

I would have really liked to retreat to the third grade where I could've called him a "big stupid head" and stomped off to play with my toys by myself. Unfortunately, I saw the logic in his statement, but I'm not a rational sort of girl, so I gave him the finger and dropped down into a chair to do some pouting of my own.

He all but threw himself on the couch across from me, crossed his arms, and sat there glaring at me in a way that I should *not* have found attractive at all. Unfortunately, I did. I found it so seriously hot that I had to pinch myself to distract myself long enough to not hop up and crawl into his lap. Lap crawling was simply not a good strategy and I desperately needed to reassert myself before things got completely out of hand.

"You know," he started with a tilt of his head. "You're really sexy when you're pissed. I always thought that was sort of a cliché, but not so much."

I blew air out between my lips and rolled my eyes to deflect attention from how pleased I was with his compliment. There was really only one thing that could be said in the face of such a stupid thing. "Fuck you."

He laughed, clearly still frustrated. "Fuck you right back, lady."

Was "lady" a step up from "woman"? I frowned at him as he dropped his head back against the couch and closed his eyes. He looked defeated. It wasn't a good look at all and I knew I'd done that to him. He wasn't playing the game right—because no one was supposed to *lose* at this game.

He wanted more. It was practically an alien concept. When had we stopped being fuck buddies? Caleb Howard had always had the ability to utterly decimate his opponents on the field and I had a feeling the running back had decided that I was a full-on, in-his-face opponent. I wondered if I should put on protective gear. I had a helmet from when I'd dated the professional skateboarder who had forced me into a pair of Rollerblades one day. I shuddered at the hellish memory of that. It had taken me five seconds of rolling terror to realize that no matter how fantastic his dick was and how well he used it, no man was worth that much sacrifice on my part.

I focused on Caleb, taking in his sprawling six-foot frame with a shrewd attention to detail. He probably weighed two hundred pounds and his sleekly muscled body was damn near perfection in motion—on the field and in bed. I wet my bottom lip with the tip of my tongue and then sighed. It was not enough that the man rocked my world physically. If I was going to agree to *more* I had to come up with some better reasons beyond the fact that I liked to fuck him and that I was a little bitter about waking up alone every single morning.

He was a great person. He volunteered his time in youth programs, adopted and fostered dogs. Championed programs that educated people about the evilness of dog fighting. Caleb had finished college, despite the interest that had been expressed in him by professional football recruiters starting in his sophomore year of college. I wrinkled my nose as I thought about that. If he hadn't been drafted, would he be a vet right now? I never would have met him.

"You're really going to go back to school when you retire from football?"

"Yeah. It's a . . . calling. And thanks to the money I've made playing football I can get my degree, set myself up a practice, and I'd really like to start a no-kill shelter." Caleb relaxed as he spoke; the anger seemed to drain from him with each word. He lifted his head and opened his eyes to look at me. "You confuse the hell out of me."

"Well, you're not the Mecca of clarity yourself." I took in a deep breath. "If you wanted this from me, why did you keep pretending that your best friend was actually your girlfriend? I mean, seriously, why did you?"

His mouth pressed into a thin line and his posture stiffened again. "It's all about image, right? The first time I took CeCe out, it was because one of the wives on the team kept trying to set me up with someone that I did not want to go out with. Then she sort of became my refuge from women who wanted to date me because of what I am rather than who I am. Girls that would get disappointed when they saw I wasn't wasting my money on a high-dollar house or a BMW. They expected me to roll like money would never stop coming."

"Yeah, I get that."

I'd certainly encountered my share of women like that in the time that I'd worked as a PR agent for professional athletes. In fact, girlfriends, wannabe girlfriends, and wives were often stumbling blocks. Too many extra women throwing themselves at money, too many parties, a wife who got vicious or disillusioned with each new dollar her man made . . . well, it was a recipe for disaster. A disaster that unfortunately happened a lot.

"So."

Fuck. I really hated this. It made me resent the fact that I didn't find dumb jocks attractive. Why did I have to pick out sexy and *smart* men to hook up with? Why couldn't he be emotionally unavailable, commitment phobic, and thinking with his cock? I shuddered at the thought of that; I'd never spread my legs for a man like that and I damn well knew it.

At twenty-eight years old I should have had a pretty good idea of what I wanted. It couldn't be that hard to find personal truth. I've never lied to myself, not even when it would have been easier and less painful to do so. Granted, personal reflection hadn't ever been on my list of fun things to do, but surely I was capable of it.

"So," he said again.

"Pushy much?" I demanded and frowned at him. "This isn't the kind of thing that I can just make a snap decision about."

"Oh, really? Christ on a crutch, Sonya! We've been doing *this* for two damn years. You mean to tell me in all that time you never once wanted more from me—and really, if you don't want a relationship with me . . . and we *'just fuck'* . . . why exactly are you pissed off that I never spend the night?"

I'm never dating a smart man again. Maybe I won't even date any more men at all. The fuckers. Every one of them is just a big, ugly mess waiting to happen. I hated nothing like a mess. We had a mess at work and I had a mess at home. I needed a bottle of wine, a long bath, and an orgasm. Since I'd pretty much promised Tara I wouldn't drink my troubles away, my entire fantasy was ruined.

I stood from my chair, shrugged out of the lightweight jacket I'd kept on when I arrived, walked to stand in front of him, unceremoniously unhooked the button that kept my halter dress on, and let it slither to the floor in a linen heap around my platform sandals. His gaze drifted over my bare breasts, to the barely there panties, straight down my legs to the clunky white sandals.

He cleared his throat. "If I asked you to keep the shoes on . . ."

"I'd know you were a total freak." I slipped out of the thong, tossed it aside with one foot, and crawled right into the lap I'd been avoiding. "I don't know what I want, Caleb. I don't know where I want this thing between us to go. What I do know is that I want you. I've wanted you since the moment I set eyes on you. *You* changed the rules of our little game, altered the rules of engagement right out from underneath me, and I've spent the last two days trying to figure out where this all fits together. So give me a break, here."

Caleb slid his hands up my thighs and spread his legs, spreading mine in the process. "Yeah, okay. I think I can swing that." He cupped my hips and pulled me closer with a soft exhalation. "Girl, you've got no idea what you do to me."

Carefully, he rubbed the lips of my bare sex with his thumbs and sucked on his bottom lip. I hissed as he spread me open, his eyes focused on the soft, pink flesh of my pussy. Clenching my hands against his shoulders, I endured his playful exploration and shuddered only minimally when he slid one large, blunt finger into me. I couldn't help but clench around the invasion.

"So fucking hot," he murmured as he pulled his finger free. His gaze met mine as he sucked his finger into his mouth.

I couldn't help but moan as I watched him suck my juices off his finger with all diligence. He laughed softly and ran both hands up my rib cage to cup my breasts. My nipples tightened further against his fingers and I swallowed a groan as he pinched them. The sharp pain was delicious but not too much. No, Caleb always skirted the edge very well.

He pulled me closer and latched onto one aching breast with his mouth. It was more than I could take in silence. I groaned and let my head fall back in utter surrender. I cupped the back of his head with one hand and shuddered through each lash of his tongue and the gentle pull of his lips. How could I give this up? Hell, why did I want to give this up?

Nails scored down my back and I went for his belt. There is only so much a woman can be expected to endure. He released my nipple but caught it briefly with his teeth and then relaxed back on the couch as I fumbled with his belt. Caleb chuckled and plucked up both of my hands. He pressed one kiss into my left palm and grinned. "Such a needy girl. What am I going to do with you?"

"Fuck me into the mattress," I answered immediately.

"Yeah, that sounds like a plan. I can always count on you to have a plan."

He slid forward, cupped my ass, and urged me against him. I gasped a little as he stood but hurriedly wrapped my legs around his waist. "A little warning would have been nice."

"Oh, girl, I'm finished giving you warnings." He walked into my bedroom and crawled up onto the bed. I gasped as he laid me down. "From now on, my playbook is going to be a complete mystery to you."

I laughed. That wasn't nearly as frightening as I thought it should have been. He brushed his mouth over mine briefly and then lifted away. I watched through barely open eyes as he slid off the bed and quickly undressed. Each article of clothing that dropped onto the floor was a relief. I don't know that I could have stood a repeat performance of the night before.

He picked up one of my feet, unbuckled my sandal, pulled it off, and dropped it onto the floor. He was utter hell on my shoes. I really should've been upset about that. Caleb tossed the second one over his shoulder, keeping his fingers around my ankle as he moved back onto the bed. He spread me wide with firm hands and then sat back on his heels to look at me.

"What?"

"You're just so fucking fine," he muttered with a sigh. "I think you'll be the death of me."

I grinned. "I'll keep you safe." Lifting my hips, I watched his tongue dart out to wet his bottom lip. "Eat me."

"Is that what you want?"

"Yeah, fuck me with your tongue."

He laughed, silky, soft, and full of promise. Caleb ran both of his big hands up my legs and lowered his mouth. The first flick of his tongue across my clit made it pulse and harden. I relaxed and let myself get lost in the soft, wet heat of his mouth. He sucked and licked at my clit until I was moving against his mouth trying to get more of the heady pleasure he offered without pause.

When I thought I could take no more of it, he moved lower and pushed his tongue into me. The shallow penetration was so startling and powerful that I nearly came. I rubbed the back of his head in shock and in something close to despair. I suddenly, really, resented every single second of my life that I hadn't spent with him. He cupped my ass with both hands. I hissed my displeasure when his tongue slid out of my pussy.

"Teasing bastard."

He laughed against my heated flesh and lifted away. "We need a toy."

"Oh." I wiggled my eyebrows. "Now we're talking."

I watched him slide off the bed and go to my dresser. The bottom drawer housed the toys and various other things that we'd played with in the past two years. He pulled out a butterfly vibrator and a bottle of lube. I relaxed on my elbows and rubbed my thighs together briefly as I looked him over. The man was gorgeous with clothes on, but he was a work of art naked. Strong, leanly muscled, beautiful dark mocha skin, a thick cock that made my mouth water: he did it for me six ways from Sunday. I licked my lips.

He grinned. "You want to suck me?"

"Absolutely." A very dirty part of me wanted him to use me: fuck my mouth with that big gorgeous cock of his. I'm a needy but lucky girl because he crawled up onto the bed and laid on his side beside me. I turned on my side and immediately latched onto the head of his cock. Pre-cum drenched my tongue and I sucked eagerly before taking as much of him into my mouth as I could. The large, blood-dark head of his dick brushed against the back of my throat as he thrust gently into my mouth again and again.

I barely noticed him sliding the toy into place, fitting it snug against my clit. He tightened the soft leather straps that would keep the toy in place and flicked it on. I released his cock from my mouth with a startled sound.

"Wow."

He laughed. "You know what I want."

"Oh, yeah."

"Turn over so I can play with your pretty ass."

I immediately rolled to my knees, stumbling just briefly as the butterfly toy slid against my clit. I rested my arms on the bed and let my head lay in my open hands as he positioned himself behind me and rubbed my ass with both hands. We didn't do anal a lot but he was a complete pro at it. I never had to worry that he would hurt or misuse me this way.

I giggled a little when his lips brushed over the small of my back and then cried out wordlessly as he upped the intensity of the vibrations on my clit. He dropped the remote on the bed beside me and picked up the lube. I was in for a wild ride and I could hardly wait for it. I pushed back shamelessly against his fingers as he brushed them over my anus. The cool, slick lubrication started to warm almost immediately. The friction of his fingers on my skin caused it to heat and tingle. He breached me with one finger and I tried to concentrate on that rather than the toy that was industriously working my clit. My whole body was primed for a long, hard fuck and I didn't want to come before he was in me. He opened me with gentle but insistent fingers.

I rocked into his invading fingers, my breath coming in short, harsh gasps. It had been a really long time since we'd done this. Long enough that it was going to hurt a little and the thought of that quick pain and then the pleasure that would follow was enough to make my eyes cross.

Finally, when I was certain that begging was on my agenda, he pushed into me in one hot, hard thrust. I moaned into the mattress beneath us and shook with pleasure and pain. All of it was delicious, overwhelming, and sated something deep inside me that I didn't want to name.

"Yes." I pushed back against him as he started to move. "Fuck. God. Yes."

Caleb fumbled for the remote control and soon had the butterfly toy humming at maximum intensity on my clit. He powered into me with long, steady thrusts that were so intense that we'd both fallen away from words completely. All we had left were moans and ragged breaths that did nothing but communicate the most basic of needs.

His hands gripped my hips as he increased our pace, pulling me back against his groin with each move he made—reminding me, owning me. A sob caught in my throat as orgasm started to rush against my already overloaded senses. The skin on my back chilled, my muscles tightened in anticipation, and I clenched my fists into the comforter underneath us as I gave in to it. The walls of my vagina clenched around nothing, juices flowed in a rush of wetness and heat, and I screamed as he thrust deep inside one last time.

"Fuck." He rested his head against my back and shuddered. "Just fuck."

He was gone when I woke up. But, he left a note. It was the first time he'd ever bothered with such a thing, but it didn't make up for the fact that he was gone. He had a team meeting he couldn't miss; I understood that on a rational level. But on another, more basic level I was hurt and furious. I couldn't very well expect the man to disregard his responsibilities in order to deal with me and my ridiculous abandonment issues.

Hell on Earth began shortly after I arrived at work. Tara was at her desk, still doing her damnedest—and failing—to get a meeting with Jean Turst, the reporter who had outed her relationship with Joshua Keller. I'd known Tara since junior high school, so I knew how well she took failure, which was to say not at all. In high school she would have been voted "the person most likely to be absolutely perfect or die trying" if such a category had existed.

Kristen Travis, our third partner in business and sometimes dubious operations that might have been considered crimes by less enlightened people, was at her desk—moody and well into her fifth day of a "big fat pity party." "She'd been that way ever since she'd come across the reporter and had accidently given a statement that had all but told the world that Tara was, in fact, fucking a client. Tara had taken the situation in good grace but Kristen had climbed up on the cross.

The hellish portion of my day had arrived about halfway through my first venti café latte, which was sacrilegious. CeCe Richards strolled into our offices like she'd been there a hundred times when in fact she'd never even set foot in the building. The look she sent me made me want to check and make sure my skin wasn't falling off.

"CeCe." I raised an eyebrow and glanced at the rolled-up newspaper she had in hand. "Caleb didn't mention you might stop by."

"He doesn't know." She tossed the paper onto the desk in front of me, sprawled messily across my keyboard. "I look like a fool."

I sighed and organized the paper so I could see what she was talking about. The headline in the "social section" was enough to make my mouth drop open. I cleared my throat. "'Caleb Howard makes first-time public appearance with longtime lover, Sonya Carson.'" The byline was familiar. "Jean Turst strikes again."

"Goddamn it!" Tara sat back in her chair dejected. "What the hell did we do to this woman, seriously! Did one of us steal her boyfriend or maybe her favorite jeans or something in college? I just don't fucking get it."

I scanned the article and felt my cheeks flush with heat. "So I'm a whore."

CeCe sighed. "I told Caleb it was a mistake for me to go to all those parties and things with him."

I sighed. "Jeez, you know he's going to flip his lid." I motioned her to sit. "So why did you?"

"Because he got tired of all those fresh young things that may or may not be legal trying to crawl into his lap." CeCe shrugged. "It seemed like the solution since the two of you were being idiots."

I glared at her. "I'm not an idiot."

"I could take a poll," CeCe offered with a small smile. "I'm pretty sure letting your man pretend to date another woman might rank up there with some pretty stupid things."

I wanted to shoot her the bird, but she was Caleb's best

friend and one of the few people on earth that he really trusted and cared for. "Okay, so I'm a whore and an idiot and I stole *your* man."

She started laughing. She had a great laugh, full of genuine amusement and goodness. I'd never known her to be anything but kind and generous to the people around her. She certainly didn't deserve to be in the middle of this. I looked toward Tara, who had slumped down in her chair a little, furious but thoughtful.

"Well, did one of us really mess her over in college?"

"She dated that guy named Mark." Tara raised an eyebrow. "The one that followed Kristen around and acted like the world existed for the sole purpose of her birth. Remember? I think he dumped Jeannie senior year because Kristen and Joel had broken up."

Kristen groaned and dropped her head onto her desk. "He did. Mark dumped her right after they'd decided to get engaged. That guy came running to me when he found out I was single and told me we were soul mates." She lifted her head and frowned. "He offered me the same engagement ring he'd just taken off her finger."

"Asshole," CeCe muttered. "She should consider herself lucky that she escaped that jerk."

"But, that can't really be it. I mean, if that was it, wouldn't she have started with me?" She flushed and looked down at her desk. "I mean, I'm not having hot kinky sex or anything but it's not like I don't have a secret or two she could expose."

I grinned. "Are you implying, dear one, that I'm having kinky sex?"

She blushed. "Yeah."

Everyone laughed and I sat back in my chair and tried to look wounded. I glanced back down at the article about Caleb and sighed. "I don't even have the faintest clue as to how we can explain this. I mean, the article all but says I'm a man-stealing slut."

"Don't forget the part where I'm a fool who can't keep a man."

"Sorry, CeCe."

"Not your fault. I'm the idiot who went along with his silliness. He should have just started dragging your narrow ass to parties against your will so I wouldn't have to play his buffer against gold-digging sports groupies."

"My ass is not *narrow*."

"Girl, please, how much do you weigh?"

I blushed. "122."

"*Narrow*," CeCe repeated with a grin. "Cute, though. I always thought you were a good choice for him. It helps that you have your own job and money."

I leaned forward and rested my chin on one hand, my elbow comfortable on my mouse pad. "So, this new guy you've got your eye on. Does he know the truth?"

"Yeah. He knows. He was a little stunned at first but I had him and Caleb over for dinner a month ago and we got all of that settled."

"Good." I crossed my arms. "At least I'm not a gold-digging, man-stealing slut."

CeCe chuckled. "Oh, well, you know, I'm sure someone will get around to comparing your financial assets soon enough."

"Okay, here's the thing." Kristen stood up and brought a folder over to my desk. "Caleb has never once said you were his girlfriend, CeCe. He's always referred to you as his best friend." She laid out several articles. "Never once in print or in television interviews has he said that you were romantically involved."

"I know." CeCe spread out some of the articles. "He never wanted to lie to people. We just let everyone draw conclusions."

"So, I'm going to talk to him and then I think we'd be comfortable drafting a statement from you. I know Julie Caldwell from the *Times*. I can get her to do a little piece on you and your work in the city. You can be quoted on the subject and clearly define your relationship. This will be good for your image and it will firm up the fact that Caleb has never claimed that you were a romantic partner." Kristen leaned back in her chair with a little frown as she considered her plan of action.

CeCe smiled. "You are his PR agent, not mine."

"My allowing him to get away with a beard for two years created this situation—and now I'm going to fix it." Kristen crossed her arms. "Of course, I thought he was gay. I had no idea he was just . . ." she waved her hand in my direction and I pushed back a snotty response.

"Fucking me?" I questioned. Okay, so I didn't get the snotty response pushed down far enough.

She blushed. "I was *not* going to say that."

"Right," I said slowly and grinned. "You hardly ever use the word *fuck*."

"You suck." She went back to her desk and pointedly turned her back on me. Her perfect little fingers flew over her keyboard. "I'll have you know I use the word *fuck* all the time. I'm a professional at using the word *fuck*."

Silence reigned for nearly thirty seconds and then we all started laughing—really, really hard. The elevator dinged and the doors slid open to reveal Caleb and his agent. He looked guilty as hell and more than a little pissed off. His gaze darted from my face to CeCe's and then back to mine.

"Hey."

"Don't mind us," I said with a little smile and a wave. "We're having our secret girlfriend/put-upon best friend of Caleb Howard monthly meeting." CeCe snickered and he glared at us both.

"Kristen is working on a society piece for CeCe and she'll draft a statement for you as well."

"And you?" he asked with a frown. "How are we going to address what they are saying about you?"

I picked up my ink pen and tapped it on the surface of my desk. "Look, it's hardly the first time I've been accused of taking some woman's man. The fact is that I'm fine. Everyone either wants me, hates me, or wants to be me." I raised one professionally arched eyebrow and grinned. "It's a real trial being this hot."

"I bet." CeCe patted my arm. "Let me know my part, ladies. I'm off to lunch. The women in my office are trying to cheer me up since I was apparently dating an asshole."

Caleb groaned. "Ce!"

"Hey, I get a few meals out of this and maybe a long lunch hour to shop." CeCe grinned. "This fine woman you're *dating* and the woman you pay to keep your ass looking like a prince are going to settle this up for me."

"Yeah, and if that doesn't work out we can always fall back on plan B." I glared at the newspaper still in my lap.

"What's plan B?" Kristen asked, turning abruptly in her chair to stare at me.

"Operation Kick Jean Turst's Ass." I really meant it. Of course, they all laughed like I wasn't capable of it. "Hey, I could totally kick her whiny ass."

"Sure, sure." Tara waved me off. "You're the epitome of badass."

The real problem with my situation wasn't that Caleb wanted something that I couldn't give. I just didn't think I wanted to give it. He wasn't playing by my rules and he'd started calling me on my bullshit. Sabotaging relationships has always been more of a craft than a mere hobby with me and I knew it. There wasn't a single man in my past who I hadn't basically run all over and left holes in. If I were going to be all weepy about it, I'd blame my father. After all, the man did walk out on me when I was ten, leaving me with a mother who found her thrills at the bottom of a bottle and in the arms of stranger after stranger.

Still, having a fucked-up childhood and parents that would never be June and Ward Cleaver was really no excuse for me using men like sex toys. I liked Caleb Howard a lot more than I should have and I resented it. I resented him. The afternoon at work had been full of dealing with the latest "sex scandal" that was directly related to the three of us. It felt really personal now and it was potentially damaging to our image and the company's bottom line. Tara's ambition and money had founded the Marcus Group but I'd certainly done my part to make it successful. I hated the idea of someone messing with it.

In the end, I hadn't turned up much more on Jean Turst than Tara's father had. Of course, he'd given us a lot of information but nothing juicy enough to get her to leave us alone and that's what we needed. As it was, the woman was making a career off our love lives and that irked me on an entirely new level. I would have loved to sit on my couch and plan mayhem and chaos all night but I'd stupidly agreed to go out to dinner with Caleb under the watchful eyes of my two best friends. If I'd told him no, I would have endured a situation not unlike the Spanish Inquisition, and no woman should have to suffer such a thing without a way out. It had all happened two hours before lunch, for fuck's sake.

I took a quick shower, freshened up my hair, reapplied my makeup, and found a dress to wear that wouldn't allow a bra. Any excuse was a good excuse to forget the bra. I was in the middle of picking out shoes when he strolled into my bedroom looking all slick and GQ in a dark suit. With some people, money made them look good. Then there were people like Caleb who made money look good. He was effortlessly beautiful and graceful. It was sort of disgusting.

"Wear the black strappy ones."

"No way." I waved him off. "You are too hard on my shoes and those things cost entirely too much to be tossed aside by you a couple of hours from now. For a man whose job it is to catch and run with the ball, you sure do a lot of throwing."

He laughed. "Come on, they make your legs look fantastic."

That was enough to make me put them on. I buckled them with steady fingers and then glared at him. "If you throw them and they get scuffed I'll never forgive you and neither will Jimmy."

"Jimmy?"

"Choo. He would be most upset to learn how little regard you have for his shoes." I checked my hair in a mirror and then grabbed my purse. "Where are we going?"

"Just dinner. I figured we could use a night out and hiding isn't productive."

I sighed. Kristen had told him that before he'd left our offices. She'd been adamant that he not respond to the newspaper story directly but through our offices and that he go on about his life as usual. So, when he'd turned to me and asked me about dinner later all I could do was say yes. I had no damn clue what I wanted from him and that was really starting to irk the hell out of me.

Dinner hadn't been a disaster but we'd been subjected to quite a few stares and he'd signed a few autographs while I got "oh, that's the white girl" looks from some of his female fans. It was no less than what I expected and oddly by the time he drove into the parking lot near my apartment building and parked I was well on my way to an amused indifference. It was

pretty damn hard to be pissed off about the attitudes of a bunch
of people I didn't even know when he was right there in my life
making things interesting and sexy.

He allowed himself to be lead up to my apartment with an
amused little smile on his lips. I figured he was up to something
and all I could really hope was that it was terribly naughty and
I'd have a starring role.

"Tell me what you want."

I frowned at him. "World peace, a strong economy, and gas
under two dollars a gallon."

He glared at me, his gaze narrow. "Christ, were you a
beauty queen in high school or something?"

I flushed. "I may have been Miss Peaches and Cream."

Caleb stared for a second and then laughed softly. "Wow."

"Shut up." I tossed my purse and then carefully pulled my
own shoes off despite his frown. "Don't even, big guy; I'm
tired of you throwing my shoes around. You've scuffed two
pair this week alone and that is just . . . frankly, I'm starting to
consider your treatment of my shoes acts of attrition."

"I see." He glanced me over. "So, should I start peace nego-
tiations or would you like to move straight into the reparations
stage?"

"That depends."

"On what?"

"Where do you have to be tomorrow morning?"

"Early practice."

"And you didn't pack a bag."

He frowned at me. "No."

"Then we'll have to call in a third party for peace negotia-
tions and you can go home." I plucked out my earrings as I
walked down the hall to my bedroom. "Good night, Caleb."

"You suck."

"I sure would have," I called out sweetly. "Thought about it all day, actually, sucking that pretty cock of yours." I laughed at his loud groan. "Sweet dreams."

"Come put the chain on before you go to sleep, babe."

4

There are worse things than going to sleep alone. I knew that. I'd been living it for two years and I knew I only had myself to blame. It's a pretty horrible moment in a girl's life when she realizes she's the source of her own misery. Selfish little bitch that I was, I wanted Caleb in my life on my terms, not his. I didn't want a discussion. I didn't want to have an adult conversation that resulted in a definition of roles and relationship perimeters.

In short, I wanted him in bed when I went to sleep and when I woke up but that screamed *relationship* and I hadn't done something that stupid since college. A series of failed relationships had taught me that men were really good for bed sport but I never failed to get burned if I took a man too seriously. My arrangement with Caleb wasn't exactly perfect since I wasn't getting everything I wanted due to my own sabotage. Of course, by keeping him off balance I was preventing him from really pushing us both in the direction that he wanted.

I've never been the kind of woman who would withhold sex as some kind of power play. Sex is about pleasure and fun. It's about connecting with your partner and getting the most of your experiences with them. It's not a tool, at least it never has been for me. Yet, I'd basically kicked Caleb out of my apartment rather than sleep with him when he'd made it clear he would have to leave and go home. I had tossed and turned all night, which made me wonder just how long Caleb usually lingered with me in the early morning hours before he left for whatever task lay ahead of him.

He'd said that I wasn't going to get to look at his playbook anymore; it was startling to realize that I didn't even have a playbook. I had learned early in life how to keep a man interested, off balance, and pleasured. I was good at it. I was more than good at it, and a part of me was admittedly disgusted by that self-evaluation. But if he wasn't playing the same game as I was, I really had no clue how I was going to control the man. I was essentially screwed and not in that magically delicious way.

As if my morning wasn't going to be complete without a hassle, I had to wait in line at Starbucks for thirty minutes before I could even place my order. When it was my turn I ordered something sweet, complicated, loaded with caffeine, and utterly bad for my figure. Maybe it was time to add a little padding to my apparently *narrow* ass. When I returned to my car I found a woman leaning against it and immediately recognized Jean Turst from the pictures Tara's father had forwarded to us.

Her hair was up in a tidy bun on top of her head like an older woman and it looked totally out of place on a woman I knew to be twenty-eight years old. Her clothes were definitely something an older woman would wear. I tried to think back to college to see if I could remember if she had always dressed like a middle-aged woman but the information totally escaped me.

"Ms. Turst, how can I help you?" I balanced my coffee in one hand with my purse as I used my remote to open my car. "I'm not prepared or willing to give statements on clients with the Marcus Group in the Starbucks parking lot."

She smirked. "How does it feel for everyone to know you're a whore?"

"Pretty cool, actually. I've always enjoyed getting my picture in the paper and I'm very attractive so I don't really have a bad side. The picture in the *Times* was truly one of the best I've had taken of me in recent years. You have to admit I looked fine in that dress." I tossed my purse into my car and turned to smile at her. "How does it feel to be you? Lonely, with a crap career writing social columns? I would think a woman of your educational background would be more interested in real news and not stuff that belongs in a tabloid. Do get your ass off my car; I'm still making payments on it and I can't afford body work and keep myself in new shoes at the same time."

She flushed blood red and straightened away from my car. "You think you are so funny."

"Yep, and smart."

"You're not better than me. You're just a whore with an alcoholic mother and father who couldn't bother to stick around and raise you. How does that make you better than me?"

My stomach clenched briefly. Little Jean had certainly grown claws since college, that was for certain. "You are a very sad person, Jean Turst, and I really pity you." I slid into my car, jerked the door shut, locked it, and drove away quickly.

I was still shaking with anger and hurt when I got to the office, so when I walked in I was relieved to see I was the first to arrive. I tossed the six newspapers I'd bought that morning before my Starbucks run and took them apart, separating the society and sports pages for each one so that we could look them over as a group for articles on our clients—good and bad. After I got the papers sorted, I turned on my computer and started my automatic search program for all of our clients. One of the first things I'd done when we'd started the Marcus Group was to build our own search engine so we could monitor major news sites, blogs, forums, newsgroups, and so on, for information on our business and the athletes that we represented.

I was nearly calm enough by the time Tara arrived because she took one look at me and dropped her briefcase. I winced and started to stand to help her but she waved me off and retrieved the abused case from the floor.

"What the fuck is wrong with you?"

"Jean Turst cornered me at Starbucks this morning—called me a whore, my mother an alcoholic, and my father a deadbeat. Just normal stuff."

Tara flushed with anger. "Why the hell doesn't she come at me? I mean, seriously? She attacks my business, my client first, and then immediately corners Kristen. Now she's stalking you at Starbucks, for fuck's sake?"

"If she has a plan . . . Kristen is next." I tried to relax in my chair. "I mean, she's managed to pretty much rip you and me both a new one in the press. I can't figure out how she knew that you were interested in Joshua. I mean, how could she have known that going after him would make you vulnerable?"

Tara sighed and pulled open a desk drawer. She brought a folder to me and opened it. It was a picture of her at a party taken several months before and Joshua was next to her—they were talking, heads tilted close together. It was clear that they were attracted to each other and pretty much oblivious to everything else in the room around them. "Huh."

"Yeah." Tara sighed. "I've been thinking the same thing for a while. So I started going through press pictures that might have appeared in the paper that Turst works for. I found this one and a few more. . . ." She flipped to the next picture. Joshua was a few feet away from her looking at her like she was his last meal on Earth. "I remember this party, and for the life of me it never once crossed my mind that he wanted me; but looking at this picture . . ."

I sighed. "Yeah. Geez." I flipped to the next one and they were dancing at the same party. He had one hand on the small of her back, his face tucked close, his eyes closed. "He's in love with you."

"Yeah." Tara nodded.

"Mutual?"

"Yeah. Crazy, right?"

"Not crazy—very cool. You both deserve something good out of this mess, and isn't it a kick in the pants that you like to get all tied up and spanked and he likes to do it?" I grinned when she blushed. "Seriously, that's *fate.*"

She leaned against the desk. "She really mentioned your mom?"

"Yeah." I swallowed hard. "You know, I spent a lot of my life separating myself from that situation but it's never been any grand secret. I did an essay on it in college that got published in the college newspaper so I don't know why I was so startled and freaked out that she said that to me. I succeeded in spite of a crappy-ass childhood and I shouldn't feel the need to defend myself from that crap." I waved my hand as I spoke. "If I get upset she wins."

The elevator doors opened and Kristen came in dragging a briefcase on wheels behind her. I frowned at her. "What have you been up to?"

"This is all the stuff I have from college: the little newspaper, yearbooks, pictures, etc. Everything. It's obvious that our problem with this woman started a long time ago and I figured it might help jog some memories. I really don't think this is about a guy. I really don't. I mean, maybe if I'd actually dated him or married him I could see how she might hate me but I don't think she ever even realized he tried to get with me after he broke up with her." She pulled the case over to the large work table and sat down in a chair. "We need to figure this out and shut her down because—not to be unfeeling or anything—I'm the next target and I'd rather not have my personal life be fodder for the social column."

I grinned. "What personal life? You're married to your job."

She blushed. "I have a personal life. I mean . . . there is stuff I'd rather no one know and Jean seems to be pretty damn good at finding stuff out. Ever since this thing started I've been trying to figure out where she would dig next and since she contacted me I'd sort of assumed I'd be next. It never occurred to me that she would latch onto you."

"Well, I gave her the rope on that front; she just had to do a little jig under my swinging body." I waved my hand as I spoke. "Anyone in my apartment building could have seen Caleb coming or going. She could have gone door to door and found someone willing to gossip to her. It wasn't like we were playing *Mission: Impossible* or anything when he came over."

Tara sat down at the table and watched Kristen unload the material from her briefcase into careful little stacks. Pictures, yearbooks, and the bimonthly newspaper from our college soon filled up the space. "So, what can we expect from you, Kris? Got any secret lovers or anything lurking around in the dark?"

Kristen blushed. "No. I'm not seeing or sleeping with anyone. In fact, I haven't even gone out on a date in a year—which is embarrassing enough in itself. But I doubt it's juicy enough to warrant time in the social column. There are plenty of women in Atlanta who aren't dating." She flushed. "But, there are other things I'd rather no one know."

Call me curious but she was getting redder by the minute and nothing was more fascinating that our dear friend at that very moment. I leaned in. "What? Come on, we can't prepare if we don't know what could come at us."

"I write." She sat back in her chair. "You know I used to write for the newspaper and I shared a few creative writing classes with Jean in school. That's why I was so surprised when I didn't recognize her. I mean, I spent time with her; I should have recognized her."

"You write," Tara repeated. "Like . . . what?"

"I just write. I have a Web site online that I use to publish short stories and there has been some interest from an agent. It's not anything, really, just a hobby more than anything."

"Do you sell your work online?" I asked and then leaned forward. I wondered briefly if I'd read anything she'd written, but then dismissed it because I bought most of my erotica online and I couldn't imagine sweet little Kristen writing dirty stories. "I mean, are you published?"

"Yes and yes." She started to wring her hands and I glanced briefly at Tara, who was chewing her bottom lip.

"Wow." I reached out and grabbed the stack of newspapers. "So, you write what, exactly?"

"Romance."

"Erotic romance," I corrected gently. "Little inspirational romances wouldn't have you all flustered and upset. You write erotic romance."

"Yes." She closed her eyes and then dropped her head to the table with a thud. "I told you I was a professional at using the word *fuck*."

"You did," Tara responded, her voice soft and amused. "Wow. Can we read it?"

"No!" Kristen groaned. "I'm such an idiot. I don't know what I was thinking. I mean, it was just supposed to be a hobby but I joined this writing group and then suddenly I was putting this Web site together and publishing my little stories myself."

"How much money have you made?" Tara asked with a little grin.

"Enough that I had to register a business name and file taxes last year." She lifted her head, her dark brown eyes were wet with tears. "I've worked really hard to keep it a secret, Tara. I would never want to embarrass you."

Tara frowned. "I'm not embarrassed, really. How bad could it be?"

"Worse than if you'd actually been having sex in those pictures with Joshua," Kristen declared, miserable. "I'm a porn peddler, for the love of God. My mother will kill me!"

"Oh, you are not writing or selling porn." I waved her off, confident that she wasn't capable of anything so deliciously bad. "Erotic romance is not porn. It's . . . romance with naughty words and explicit sex. It's about strong, powerful women getting what they want from a man. You have nothing to be ashamed of." I tilted my head. "Just how much money have you made?"

"Enough." She crossed her arms and looked away. "It's bad, okay? I mean, it's really bad. How do you think our clients would treat me if they knew I wrote stuff like that?"

"I don't know." I glared at her. "Maybe they would insinuate that you should fuck them as part of the contract."

Kristen sighed. "Yeah, exactly—just like Davis did you. Then what? Both of you would be painted with the same brush as me and it's bad enough what has already happened. Just how much more crap do you think we can take before people start looking at us like we have a serious problem? Tara is a slut who likes to be spanked, you're a gold-digging slut who can't be trusted around men, and I'm going to be an Internet porn queen."

"Gold digging?" I demanded.

"Page four, *Tribune*." Tara smiled sadly. "I see you haven't gotten through the papers this morning."

"Fuck me." I propped up my hand on my chin and stared at Kristen. "So, I assume you write under a pen name?"

"Yes, of course." She glared at me. "No, I'm not ready to say what it is."

I grinned at her. "Have I bought from your Web site? Because I buy most of my erotica online. It saves me from getting lectures at the bookstore from well-meaning but ridiculous clerks who think I give a fuck what they think about my reading habits."

"I don't really know. I try not to look at the names of people who buy, just in case I meet them by accident or something." She stood and walked away from the table. "I've done my best to hide my identity within the company but if someone was diligent they could certainly figure it out. Nothing can really be a secret. I've been tempted to just dismantle the whole thing but it's big enough that if I tried to, it might cause more of a situation."

I stared at her for a second. "Tell me."

"No."

"Kristen." I frowned at her. "You can trust us and I would never judge you for this. Tara has no room to judge you for it."

"Hey!" Tara shot me a look. "You're not some sweet little virgin yourself."

"Please, the kinkiest thing I do is a few sex toys and anal sex." I waved her off and blushed when Kristen laughed. "What?" I sighed. "Okay, I might have had a threesome in college and there was that one time in the tenth grade that I made out with a girl at a party. But I really don't think the girl thing is all that kinky. Everyone is entitled to an experiment or two or three."

"Oh my God."

"Seriously, Kristen. Fess up. It can't be any worse than Tara being tied to her big four-poster bed and . . ." I grinned when Tara poked me. "Seriously? Do you have any idea how hot Joshua is in my fantasy life?"

"Bitch," Tara murmured. "Your imagination can't be good enough to capture the real thing."

"Huh." I considered that for a moment. "I got waxed last

weekend. I mean . . . *waxed*. Caleb was thrilled with the result. You should try it."

"I like pain but even I have my limits," Tara muttered and Kristen jumped up and started pacing in front of us.

"It can't be that bad, Kris!"

Kristen started chewing on her thumbnail, which was stunning considering how much money she spent on her manicure. "It is. I mean it *really* is."

"Stop being a drama queen," Tara pointed to a chair. "Sit and spill."

"Lady Isabella."

Okay, so my mouth dropped open. I mean, who could blame me? I'd just found out one of my best friends really was the porn queen of the Internet. Excuse me. She was the erotic romance queen of the Internet. I visited the site all the time.

"Oh, yeah. I'm a customer." I grinned when she blushed. "Is there going to be a third book in the Slave of the Heart series because . . . damn, those werewolf brothers are hot."

She blushed. "Oh, shut up."

Who knew? Kristen Travis, PR agent by day and erotic romance author by night. The information was stunning and a little thrilling. After all, Lady Isabella specialized in books featuring ménages à trois. "So, have you ever slept with two guys at once?"

"What? No." She blushed. "It's a fantasy. That's all." She blushed and covered her face with both hands. "This is a fucking nightmare."

I stared at her a second. "That was a very professional use of the word *fuck*. I bought one of your print-on-demand books last year; if I bring it will you sign it?"

Kristen groaned. "I hate you a little right now."

5

The week passed in a blur of worry and snarkiness. To say that we were all on edge and waiting for the other shoe to drop was something of an understatement. On Thursday we'd tossed around the idea of just quietly revealing who Lady Isabella was on her Web site in the bio section. But Kristen was holding onto the idea that Jean didn't know about her and that maybe she wouldn't get hit the way Tara and I had. I didn't buy it for a second but letting her live with her delusion had made for a more peaceful work environment.

It was Sunday afternoon, and I'd spent most of the day camped out in front of my television watching the game, berating officials who could not see or hear me, calling Caleb "baby," and telling him how awesome he was. Thank God I was alone. I was genuinely mortified at myself anyway and an audience would have been more than I could stand. They won the game by the skin of their teeth so I figured it would be several hours before Caleb made it over. He'd promised to come after the game but winning with such a tight score was surely going to earn the entire team some quality time with their coach after the game.

Caleb had made noise about going out to dinner but I'd prepped food to cook. I wasn't really in the mood to be on display and I was hoping that considering his day he'd be content to just be somewhere quiet. Caleb called nearly five hours after the game to tell me he was on his way and I put the pasta on to boil. By the time he was coming in the door, I'd tossed the pasta in a chicken alfredo sauce and a salad was already on the table.

"Wow. You cooked." He pulled off his jacket and glared at me. "Christ, are you dumping me?"

"What?" I frowned at him and motioned him to sit. "Why on earth would you think that?"

"You've never cooked for me." Caleb took the wine I offered with suspicion. "I mean, we always order in and I have to go get it. If you're dumping me, could you wait until after the season? I don't think I could take it right now."

I laughed softly and wondered how many women had heard that over the years. "I'm not dumping you, jackass." I slid into my own chair. "I made you dinner because I didn't want to go out to get food and I didn't figure you would either." I raised one eyebrow and frowned at him. "You dropped the ball, sweetie. You dropped the ball twice. You need to give your fans time to recover from that disappointment before you're out in public again."

Caleb snorted. "You know what? You get hit by a collective six hundred pounds and see if you can hold onto the ball every single time. Those bastards had it in for me today." He rubbed his shoulder and sighed. "This smells great."

"It's not my job to hold onto the ball while getting leaped on by six hundred pounds of my fellow man." I patted his arm. "That's okay; I'll still have sex with you. Though, really, we should start considering your retirement options."

"Woman, you are pushing it."

I grinned. "You're twenty-eight, sweetie. That's middle age for a running back."

"I'll show you middle aged."

That was something to look forward to. We'd had a lot of private meals together, especially over the last year, and I was beginning to wonder exactly how long we'd had a very big communication problem. Or more to the point, how long I'd been punishing him for not giving me exactly what I wanted and nothing more. I had no clue when I'd become a selfish jerk but it wasn't a comfortable realization.

I set down my wineglass with a thud and winced as droplets of red wine sprinkled across my favorite tablecloth. "I'm not a nice woman."

"No?" Caleb asked with a little frown. He put his fork down. "Okay, tell me why you aren't nice."

"I'm really selfish, you know. I expect these things from you but on the other side of it I don't even know if I'm capable of giving you the things you want. I've been telling myself that I *let* you use me for sex but when it comes right down to it I think I've been trying to use you for sex and comfort but only on my own terms."

He sighed. "The first year I think it was just sex. I mean, we didn't see each other all that often and it was nice to have a woman that I trusted that I could come to for sex and no complicated crap that came with it."

"But the last year has been different."

"Yeah." Caleb admitted. "I feel like I'm spinning my wheels with you, Sonya, and I want more. I want a hell of a lot more than I can even think. I want you in my bed, I want you in my life, I want you sitting in the stadium wearing the tiniest T-shirt possible with my number blazed across it like a brand, and I want you to be *here* with me."

That was a lot. I wondered, very briefly, what the things were that he couldn't think about. Could I deal with that? Could I be on display every Sunday during football season for him? He had a few more years in the sport and then . . . well, he'd said he wanted to go back to school after football was said and done. Wasn't that fascinating? I'd always assumed with his looks and personality that we'd be able to get him into sports broadcasting after his career had run its course.

"Are you serious about school?"

"Yeah, I'd already been accepted into a vet program when I got drafted. I always had a plan B. I'm not one of those guys who viewed college as a way to play football until I got noticed." He played with his wineglass and took a deep breath. "I'm in love with you, you know that, right?"

Okay, so there are moments in a girl's life that take on this surreal fantasy-type vibe whenever she thinks about them. The first "I love you," the wedding, the moment the test tells you a baby is on the way. And then there is that moment, the moment when the man you want all of those things with makes it clear he wants those things with you, too.

"No, not really. I had no clue." I rubbed my breastbone to ease my nerves more than anything else and took a deep breath. "I sort of figured I would say it first and then you would, you know, be a man about it and I would be all hurt and disappointed. Then I would throw things at you and we'd probably have really mean sex."

Caleb laughed. "We can still have the mean sex if you want." He reached out and took one of my hands. "We haven't had mean sex since we lost to Seahawks last year."

Long live the Seattle Seahawks. I grinned as I thought about it. "Yeah, that was great." I clinched my fingers against his. "I love you. I've been afraid of it and you for a while now."

"You drive me insane but I'm really okay with that."

"Yeah?"

He pulled me a little and I gamely left my chair and slid into his lap. "Yeah, really okay with it. I figure in a few months I'm going to go to a jewelry store and buy my favorite gold digger a stupidly large diamond so that people can talk about it."

"Now that's a plan." I held out my empty hand and visualized it. "Jesus."

"Yep."

"Seriously?"

"So serious," he promised.

My life was a complicated mess but I found I really like complicated.

Double Team

1

Every woman has secrets. There are secrets so amazing and thrilling that even thinking about them can make her body rush with excitement and remembered lust. It's really too bad that most of my secrets are about dreaming instead of actually living. It had been a week since I'd "come out" to my best friends about my sideline writing career and, in spite of a few teasing comments, things had gone much better than I expected.

It was horrible of me to assume that they wouldn't understand, that they would judge me for writing about sex. Sonya and Tara had been nothing but supportive through it all but we also knew the potential for fallout to be very great. Since we'd started the Marcus Group it had been my job to be the calm, rational one. Sonya was the one who that got to have fits if something got really stupid, and Tara got denial. I was reasonable and calm. Yeah, not so much.

I sat back in my desk chair and stared at my business Web site. I'd updated the profile for Tara, the company owner, but I hadn't clicked SUBMIT yet. It was a big step, one that both Tara and Sonya had encouraged me to take. In a week, Lady Isabella was scheduled to have an interview on a local station about the success of my company and the book deal I'd just signed. It wasn't a national show but it was a preemptive strike. I wondered how Jean Turst would take it and what other dirt she had on us to throw around in public.

For the last month, Turst had done her level best to make our lives hell and we still didn't have a single clue why. She'd started with an attack on one of our most high-profile clients, Joshua Keller, and then had exposed Sonya's longtime affair with Caleb Howard. Sonya and Tara weren't convinced that she didn't have information on another client but I knew that Jean's next attack would be about me and it would be very personal.

I remembered her from college. A mousy girl with a geek boyfriend who had refused to go out with us whenever we asked and had avoided all of our events like we are passing out the plague in liquid form. The geeky boyfriend had dumped her senior year and had asked me out. I'll admit I'd been tempted to go out with him because I'd always found "smart" to be sexy but I'd been turned off by the fact that he'd dumped her just so he could ask me out. It was just really horrible. I guess I should have been flattered that he dumped her first instead of assuming that I'd go out with a guy who would cheat on his fiancée.

I stood up from my desk and plucked up my beer. I wasn't ready to submit the new bio. I was putting off the inevitable; it wasn't like I was going to be interviewed in disguise. With a sigh, I closed the browser window and walked away from my computer completely. I just wasn't ready and I really wanted to push Jean Turst off a cliff.

"I thought you were going to post the new bio last night?"

I looked up from my coffee and glanced Sonya Carson over. She had the look of a woman who had gotten everything she'd ever wanted and I figured she had. Caleb had come by three times in the last week to pick her up for lunch and the news stories about them were dying a quick death. They weren't doing anything to garner much attention and there hadn't been any semidirty pictures of them published in a tabloid—yet.

"I can't do it, not yet. I haven't even told my daddy and I really don't know how he's going to take that. I mean, geez, Sonya. My dad's a deacon in his church and my mom organized the bake sale last year. You don't know . . . these people aren't normal."

She laughed. "They sound perfectly normal to me. Look, Kris, they love you. They're family, and even if they don't approve they aren't going to shun you. You're a grown woman and you have to live your own life."

I'd been telling myself that for *years* but it was a pretty hard thing to do when you'd grown up the way I did. Sheltered would be a good term for it. I'd been a virgin until college and, while I'd shed that label pretty quickly, I'd never been as adventurous as my friends or even the women I wrote about. I'd never even had a one-night stand. Granted, I'd grown up in a time when such things were dangerous and even stupid considering the diseases out there but still—I'd never had a one-night stand. It was pathetic.

Tara strolled off the elevator looking like a million dollars and wearing a silk pantsuit that I'd seen her buy earlier in the month. Shopping was one of our hobbies and we were semi-pro at it. I grinned at that thought and then frowned when I noticed she looked irritated. "Oh, no, not again!"

"Wasn't even Jean this time." Tara tossed her briefcase onto her desk and I winced as it connected with her keyboard. "Adam McGregor and Neal Davidson."

"Neal Davidson is Sonya's client and Adam is yours." I sat up straight and went for my mouse. "Basketball. Best friends since high school?"

"Did we know that Adam is gay?" Tara asked, leaning against

her desk with her arms crossed. "Because . . . apparently he is and he's had a torrid, lifelong love affair with Neal Davidson."

Okay, so my mouth dropped open and I'm mortified to admit that I squeaked. Adam McGregor had been hitting on me for longer than he'd been a client. Officially, he was Tara's client, but it never failed that he would call the office when she wasn't in and I would end up dealing with him. I couldn't even begin to count how many times I'd turned down dinner invitations from him. Maybe he'd wanted to use me as a beard, and that was sort of insulting.

I frowned. "Wait, no, I just don't buy that. They've been friends forever but Neal is a known womanizer." I went through our database and found their profiles. "Yeah, they went to Auburn together. They were roommates through most of college and shared an apartment here for years even after they both signed . . ." I blushed. "Okay, then."

"Well, it isn't like two grown men with jobs can't be room-mates." Sonya was on the Internet looking for the story and related postings, I could tell, because all of her monitors were lit and Web sites were flying up like crazy. "I mean, well, man: they are both super hot."

I hopped out of my chair and tried not to hurry as I went to her desk to check out pictures. She was right: they were super hot and they looked fantastic together. If they were on a television show together, women all over the planet would be writing fan fiction about them getting it on because that's how hot they were. My mouth went a little dry and I blew air out between my lips. "Adam asks me out every time he sees me."

"Maybe he's bi." Sonya wiggled her eyebrows. "Maybe they'd let you watch."

"You are such a freak!" I walked away, my cheeks hot and my panties a little damp at the thought.

Tara was already on the phone with Adam and I could tell

she was doing her level best to ask him if the story was true without outright asking him if he was sleeping with his best friend. I sat down at my own desk to start reading the articles that Sonya was gathering and putting in the database. The pictures themselves weren't exactly damaging but the context of the article made them seem intimate.

Tara hung up abruptly and heaved a great big sigh. "He's on his way over here with Davidson. That picture was taken at a funeral six months ago. When Neal Davidson's father died of cancer. Now, his grief is plastered all over the Internet and being bandied about like they are having an illicit gay affair."

I looked at the picture, my stomach knotting in horror. Neal had his face buried against Adam's throat and they were holding on so tightly to each other, as if they knew that if anyone else touched them they'd fall to pieces. I didn't know how close Adam had been to the older Davidson but he didn't look like he was taking the funeral any better than Neal was. The crassness of the situation was sickening.

"And we're sure Jean isn't behind this?"

"If she did it she isn't using her name for the article and it's for a rival paper." Sonya shook her head. "And really, I don't think so. I mean, it's a sex scandal and that certainly does seem to be her favorite thing to do to us but Adam is a low-profile client and we have to force him to go to events. He just wants to play; he really isn't interested in endorsements and crap like that. Neal is in the press a lot because he likes to party and party hard but his bisexuality is by no means a secret."

It was true enough. Adam had a nice contract and great career but he wasn't interested in being in Nike commercials or selling himself for a sports drink. Money wasn't a big deal to him and everyone knew it. He did a lot for the community but didn't bank on his fame to get him anything. He was more likely to play a game of basketball with a bunch of kids from the local high school than he was to stage some photo op at a pickup game in a bad neighborhood. If he did hang out at youth centers, it was never with press coverage and he refused to talk about the money or time he gave to various charities. He was just an intensely private guy.

Neal, on the other hand, was the life of any party he showed up for but he didn't do anything stupid and he treated the people in his life well. There were never any stories about him in the papers that painted him to be an asshole or a user. He had a few mid-level endorsement deals but he always picked his products carefully.

Forty-five minutes later they came out of the elevator bickering with one another like an old married couple.

"No, absolutely not. This is ridiculous, Adam. I don't care what you have to say to the press. It doesn't matter to me."

Adam glared and jerked off his jacket with hands that were mostly not shaking. "I'm not going to stand in front of a bunch of reporters and pretend to be outraged and disgusted over the thought that people think I'm gay. That's . . . just as obscene as the story itself."

"But you aren't gay!" Neal sighed. "It's perfectly okay for you to deny that, you idiot."

"Fuck you." Adam returned. "Maybe I want to be the NBA's poster boy for gay America."

Neal laughed. "You have to be gay, first!"

"Gentlemen!" Tara tilted her head and glared at them. They both blushed and shoved their hands into their pockets, a sign of surrender if I'd ever seen it. "Come over here and sit, please."

I suppressed a laugh as they walked over to the chairs in front of Tara's desk and slouched down into them like a couple of kids who'd been called to the principal's office.

Tara sat down and inspected them both. "Now, Adam, you can't go around claiming to be gay if you aren't; that would be horrible. I realize you are both stressed out about this situation. How can we help?"

Adam sighed. "I'm not saying I want to go around claiming to be gay; that would definitely hurt my social life."

"Oh, who knows, maybe it would expand it," Sonya said cheerfully. "There are lots of great-looking men in the area and you're very pretty. You wouldn't have a problem getting a date."

"Yeah, he'd be fine until he had to put out," Neal injected, which earned him and Sonya glares from Tara.

Adam blushed. "I just . . . I'm not going to get in an interview and act like I'm disgusted by it. I don't have a problem with homosexuals . . . I just don't have a problem with it and I don't want to be perceived as some dumb jock on television acting like it's amoral to be gay."

"You aren't a dumb jock." I set coffee down in front of each of them and offered them a basket full of creamers and sweeteners. They both shook their heads and took the coffee black. "We can make this work if you'll both just calm down and let us work a little, okay?"

Adam looked over my face and I did my best not to blush under his scrutiny. He'd never hidden his interest in me and I sort of regretted always telling him no. After all, it appeared that neither Sonya nor Tara had a problem dating a client. My rule about not dating clients seemed a little stupid in the face of the great relationships I'd seen them forge recently.

"Yeah, okay, I'm listening."

Tara motioned me to continue and I propped up against her desk. "Okay, so we can release a statement explaining that the picture was taken during a funeral. If you are okay with that, Mr. Davidson?"

"Call me Neal, and yes, I'm okay with it." Neal offered me a small smile and his eyes brightened as if he were in on some little secret. His gaze traveled over me in a leisurely way that was flattering, not insulting, and he nudged Adam with his elbow. "Nice; I'd forgotten how nice the scenery is here."

Tara laughed and I blushed.

Adam ignored his friend. "So, what else?"

"We can do an interview—radio or newspaper. You can clarify your relationship with Neal and probably pull it off without discussing your sex life at all. It's really no one's business who you sleep with, anyway. At least as long as it's legal." I waved a hand. "You can, of course, categorically deny ever having had a sexual relationship with Neal without sounding like you hate gay people. It's doable . . ." I trailed off when they both blushed. "What?"

Neal sighed. "It doesn't count."

"Of course it counts," Adam said.

"I've been telling you for three years that drunken sex in Vegas does not count." Neal rolled his eyes. "We aren't even sure . . . I mean . . . you know. You were supposed to leave it in Vegas, you know. That's the rule."

Adam sighed "I woke up in bed with two naked people, Neal. I'm pretty sure I can figure out what happened." He sighed and shook his head. "Christ, I can't go on the radio and do an interview if I can't even keep my mouth shut."

"Two people?" I asked. I'm sure my eyes were huge.

Neal grinned. "Showgirl."

Sonya started laughing. "Well, they could have pictures of that . . . wouldn't that be . . ." She sighed. "I don't suppose that showgirl knew who you were? I mean, she isn't going to pop out of the woodwork and tell the world she had a threesome with you two?"

"Nah. I got Adam out of the room before she woke up and, as far as I could tell, she'd been just as drunk as we were and really didn't remember much beyond having sex with someone. Since I was the guy in the bed with her . . ." Neal trailed off and shrugged. "Doesn't matter. She might remember me but I doubt seriously she remembers Adam. I picked her up in the bar and she woke up with me."

"You know that's horrible, right?" I asked but I couldn't really frown at him; he looked so unrepentant and debauched sitting there with my favorite coffee mug, relaxed and calm while Adam was fidgetting in his chair. It occurred to me that he remembered more about that night than he was letting on. "So, you're not gay?" I asked Neal.

"Let's just say that I'm open to possibilities," he said.

"He's a whore," Adam said and Neal just laughed. "Tell me what to do, here."

"I've got a friend over at KPRX-102; she has a morning show, a pretty popular one. We can get you an interview on that show and we can prep some questions for her. She'll go along because she owes me a huge favor." Sonya refilled their coffee cups as she spoke and then topped off Tara's. "We can work this like you are what you are—very close friends with an intimate bond that is not sexual. People will certainly be on your side once they realize that picture was taken at a funeral and that it is being used in such a horrible way."

"It's a good idea," I said before Adam could protest. "You won't come off like a homophobic jerk and the public will get an explanation they can live with. Are either one of you seeing someone?" They both just smirked at me and suddenly I felt like I was in ten kinds of trouble. "Right, then; well, the interview is the way for you to go."

I looked at Neal, who was communing with his coffee, and I really couldn't blame him. It was good stuff. I'd just ground it fresh this morning. "Neal?"

"My sex life has never been much of a secret and I see no reason to justify those pictures to anyone, to be honest. It was probably the worst day of my life and I don't want to discuss that with anyone." His eyes darkened as he spoke. "I really don't."

"I understand. We can prepare a statement and release it for distribution on your behalf. Combine that with Adam's interview; that should stave off most of the discussion."

Somehow—and I'm still not sure how Sonya and Tara managed it—I ended up taking Adam to the radio station the next day. He'd sprawled in the passenger seat of my SUV as if he didn't have a care in the world and I'd spent most of the drive trying to focus on the road when all I really wanted to do was rub my hands over all six and a half feet of him. Sonya was right: Adam McGregor was a really pretty man. Dark blond hair, vivid green eyes, and broad appealing features. If the man put on a kilt and a pair of big clunky leather boots they could put him on the cover of a romance novel without a single touchup. Or he could be on one of those mostly naked covers.

Of course, once I started thinking about him being naked I was pretty much incapable of doing anything else. "Did you go over the questions and the answers we developed?"

"Yep."

"Any questions?"

"When we're done here, can I buy you lunch?"

"No. I've got a meeting with a client for lunch and then I have to run downtown for a photo shoot for Joshua Keller."

"Keller isn't Tara's client?"

"She passed him to me because of their relationship."

"Oh, yeah," Adam chuckled. "Hot pictures. They look good together, really into one another."

"They are."

"Good."

I didn't really hate her for it; Tara deserved to be happy and she deserved to be in love with a man who thought she hung the moon and stars. Joshua was absolutely stupid over her and it was obvious to anyone who managed to look their way. Their kinky bedroom antics aside, they made a great couple. Or maybe, I thought, they made a great couple because of their kinky bedroom antics. It must be a relief to be with someone who understood how to get you off and had absolutely no reservations about doing it for you.

"She's happy. I just wish the press would back off the BDSM club issue."

"It's a cool place. I don't know why everyone got all bent out of shape about it."

Thank God I was actually parking the car when he said that. I slammed the vehicle into park and glared at him. "You've been in the Playground?"

"Yeah, you haven't?" Adam laughed suddenly. "Come on, Kristen, it's one of the coolest places in town. When I got invited I nearly fell all over myself to accept. Do you know how hard it is to get into that club? You can't just walk up to the door and pay twenty bucks to get in. You've got to know someone and have a background check to be a full member with privileges for back rooms."

"Background check?"

"Yeah, the owner doesn't let anyone in to party who has a criminal background. You get searched as you enter: no outside alcohol, no drugs, and no weapons. If you get caught trying to bring that stuff in, your membership gets deleted and you're banned for life. He doesn't play about his business. It's not all BDSM either, you know. There is dancing, a really nice gaming room set up."

"So it's just a place for adults to play?"

"Yeah, and spank each other with whips if that's what they like. There are different sections. Nothing illegal goes on, as far as I could tell."

"So you've been more than once?"

"Neal's a member. I'm an associate member because I haven't joined. I think Joshua Keller is the same as me. Neither one of us could really afford to get caught on a member list for the Playground. And you know Neal could give a shit what people think of him. I think he really kind of enjoys shocking people."

We walked to the radio station in silence. He was obviously amused at my shock and I was torn between hitting him for laughing at me and crying a little for how much I'd been denying myself. Adam was really charming and fun to be around and I'd spent the last year basically telling him to get lost in a series of perfectly nice rejections. Rejections that had put most men off forever. Hell, it had been nearly two years since I'd been in a relationship with a man. I'd been hiding behind my job and my second career for a long time.

He breezed through the interview beautifully and had Sonya's friend eating out of the palm of his hand within a few minutes. I stayed the whole time, just in his line of sight but outside the studio, in case he needed my input on something. He stayed for an hour with her, talking about music, news, and just general stuff about his lifelong friendship with Neal. The loss of Richard Davidson had been a blow to them both and Adam had described the man like a second father. He talked about cancer and how important it was for men to get exams yearly for prostate health. He spoke well, never hesitated, and by the end of it even the producer who was with me was complaining about tabloids and making a profit off of people's grief.

The drive back across town didn't take as long as I would have thought and I managed to find parking only a block from the office. He walked me all the way to the building in silence. It wasn't awkward at all. Adam had never been the kind of man who had to hear his own voice all the time. It was one of the things I liked best about him. At the front doors, I stopped and turned to face him.

"You did a great job, Adam. I think this thing will die down quickly, and if we're lucky we might even get an apology out of it from the paper."

He shrugged. "I don't care about apologies. I just . . . you know that day was the worst of Neal's life. His dad fought so hard and we all thought he'd beaten it." Adam cleared his throat. "I hadn't seen Neal cry since we were in the third grade and Susanne Delmar checked the 'no' box." He smiled a little at the memory and then cleared this throat. "He doesn't deserve this. I know he acted like it didn't matter yesterday but it really messed with him that someone took that picture and made money off his grief, off his father's death."

"He doesn't blame you."

"He should," Adam snapped. "They used his father's funeral to create a scandal."

"Look, we did great damage control today and I believe the story is going to die quickly." I pulled off my gloves and tucked them into my coat pocket. "I have to run. I've got a meeting in forty-five minutes."

"Yeah. Thanks for this morning." He glanced up the side of the building. "I know they totally maneuvered you into going with me, like two little yentas."

I laughed. "Well."

"Have dinner with me?"

I wanted to say yes. I wanted to say yes in the biggest possible way but I couldn't. Jean Turst wasn't finished with us and I was next on her list. The last thing I wanted was to drag Adam into that situation, not after the day he'd just had. I didn't think he would be really upset if he knew what I wrote, but considering his own little sex scandal, I didn't think he'd want to be involved in mine.

"I want to but it probably isn't a good idea." I wet my bottom lip and watched his face for anger but all I saw was disappointment. It made me feel like a total asshole. At least if he'd gotten pissed off, I wouldn't have felt like I hurt him. "You know those stories about Tara and Sonya?"

"Yeah."

"Well, I'm probably next on the reporter's hit list. She's got some kind of personal grudge against us." I shrugged when he raised an eyebrow. "We all went to the same college. Her boyfriend had a crush on me . . . hell, I don't know. Anyway, she's been a real jerk and I don't know what she has planned for me, and I think you've got enough going on right now on the scandal front."

"I can handle it." He touched my face and I was startled by how warm his skin was, considering how freaking cold it was standing in front of the building. "I know you want me."

In the face of such arrogance, a woman should be indignant and insulted. Instead, I was mostly just insanely relieved that he knew that already. "Yeah."

He moved in closer and leaned down so he could whisper in my ear. "That story about Vegas . . . it wasn't the first time we'd shared a woman and it wasn't the last." I shivered as his hands settled on my shoulders. "If that's what you want, if you want us both . . . you can have us."

My knees went a little weak and I laughed when he caught my elbows. "Well, that's . . ."

"You don't have to pretend to be upset; it was obvious to everyone in the room that you were more interested than you were shocked." He caught my earlobe between his teeth. "That was the point, though. The whole point of bringing him with me. So you could see what we have to offer."

"Adam."

"You're picturing it in that beautiful head of yours, aren't you? Pinned between us, our hands all over you?" He pulled me close briefly. "There is *nothing* you could want that we wouldn't do for you."

I was pretty sure I was going to faint. Hell, yeah, I could picture myself in bed between them. Neal with his beautiful dark brown skin and Adam who seemed to have a perpetual tan. Both of them lean and well-muscled with big, talented hands. All of that cock just for me. *Yeah, I could picture it.* I was glad for my coat, because my nipples were so hard they hurt and the crotch of my panties was soaking wet.

"I have to go." I took a step back and a deep breath. "Check your e-mail later."

"Yeah?"

"Yeah." I smiled. "This is a little crazy."

"Life is short, Kris."

2

Life is short. It's funny how people can use that as an excuse to do things they know they really shouldn't. Rich desserts, a party on a work night, sex with a hot stranger. I was never the sort of girl who took strangers to bed no matter how tempted I might have been. Tara and Sonya had always teased me about my good-girl ways, though over the last few days they'd both started to look at me with new eyes. I knew they had a half billion questions about my writing and my side business but neither of them had really dug deep.

"So, he did well on the radio."

I nodded and then glanced up to find Tara leaning on my desk. "Yeah, he did. He also called you and Sonya a couple of yentas." I grinned when she just laughed. It was nice to see her so relaxed and comfortable, especially considering the month we'd had. "He asked me to dinner."

"And you said?"

"I told him no." I shrugged when she frowned. "Then I told him why and he said he didn't care about Jean Turst. So I told him I'd e-mail him." I wasn't up to sharing the rest of the conversation, no matter how much I'd learned about Tara and her bedroom in recent weeks. "I thought I'd set up a date for Saturday."

"After your talk-show appearance." Tara raised an eyebrow. "Giving him a chance to cut and run if he can't handle dating the Internet Porn Queen?"

"It's not porn; it's erotica!" Sonya singsonged from her desk. She wiggled her eyebrows. "And it's erotic romance if he's really good and the heroine keeps him."

I laughed softly. "Is that the way you tell?"

"It's a thin line," Sonya confided as she spun in her chair. "But I think porn has to have pictures, and cover art doesn't count."

"I love you."

She grinned. "I love you, too, sweetie. If we were both lesbians and on a cable show I'd totally chase you around until I got some."

"But only if we were on a cable show?" I asked with a frown.

"Well, yeah. In real life we'd never be friends afterward. On a cable show, we'd be best friends for life after the sex got old."

"I'll have you know I'm really good in bed. The sex wouldn't get *old.*"

"Good to know."

We all three turned at the sound of a male voice in our domain and I blushed as I caught sight of Joshua Keller leaning against the open elevator door.

He grinned. "I'll be sure to pass that info on to interested parties."

I laughed. "You'd better not."

Joshua sighed. "It'll certainly be a task to keep such amazing information to myself." His gaze followed Tara as she went to her desk to get her purse. "We have reservations in an hour— unless you want to just go home?"

"Dinner out sounds great." She stopped at my desk as she pulled on her coat. "Your interview is in three days. Stop being a big girl and update your bio on your Web site."

I crossed my arms. "I haven't even told my parents, yet."

"Yeah, well, which do you prefer? That they find out from you that you've been running a successful business in your spare time? Or do you want them to see what Jean Turst has cooked up first?"

"I think we should reconsider our plans and just let Sonya kick her ass. She said she could do it."

Sonya bounced up from her chair. "I could. I took kick-boxing lessons at the gym last year."

"You didn't learn anything," Tara reminded gently. "You were too busy staring at your instructor's ass."

Sonya dropped down in my visitor's chair and rolled her eyes. "My contributions to this team are never valued enough. To think that I spent all that time and money on kickboxing lessons and neither of you take the time to understand how truly badass I am."

"I really believe in your badassness," I promised. "Now, what do you think about going to find Jean after work and kicking her ass?"

Tara laughed. "No. Me bailing the two of you out of jail isn't the next headline I want for us."

"Yeah, well, it's better than my picture and the headline 'Internet Porn Queen Revealed' across the top of every major paper in the state."

"Erotica," Tara corrected with a little grin.

I slumped back in my chair and waved as she left with Joshua. "Is it horrible to hate her a little right now?"

"Nah, I hate her a little, too." Sonya pulled a few clips out of her pocket and pinned up her hair with a sigh. "You know, she's right. If you update your bio and keep it low key, I think the interest in the story will be minimal. But if she breaks it before you can . . . well, it'll be some dirty secret and we have enough dirty secrets around here to bandy about without adding yours to the list."

"It *is* a dirty secret," I muttered. "It's a perfectly filthy secret, actually. I never should have done it. It was stupid and vain."

"You're a gifted writer, Kristen, so don't sell yourself short."

"Yeah, well, my mom is going to blow a fucking gasket when she realizes her baby girl is writing *erotica* on the Internet."

"For all you know, she could be one of your readers. You said you never looked at the names of the people who bought from you."

"Not unless their credit transactions failed—and a lot of people use online payment services so they can hide behind business names themselves." I blushed. If my mother turned out to be a reader I would probably die of shame.

Since thinking about my mother skulking around the Internet buying erotica online was horrific, I dismissed it firmly from my mind and shut down my computer.

"You didn't cancel your dinner plans with your parents tonight, did you?"

I sat back in my chair and bit down on my bottom lip. "You don't know how much I want to. Will you go with me?"

She grinned. "Don't be a pussy, Kristen. You can't be a professional at using the word *fuck* and be afraid of your parents."

"I'm not afraid of my parents." I was afraid of my *mother*. My daddy was a walk in the park next to the force of nature that was the woman who had birthed me in the back of a mini-van twenty-nine years before.

My daddy would smirk and shake his head. My mama would have the kind of conniption fit that went down in record books as a natural disaster. I was screwed, and not in a good way.

* * *

My parents were a mixture of two entirely different cultures. My father had come from New York in the sixties for work and found himself an old-fashioned Southern belle from a prominent family to settle down with. Now, three kids and forty years of marriage later, they lived in a very nice home outside of Atlanta where they prided themselves on having the best lawn in the neighborhood and a prizewinning flower garden.

My daddy had found Jesus sometime in the nineties and my mother had been very pleased. He was a deacon in their church and that was where they spent the majority of their free time. Which meant bake sales, raffles, revivals, prayer meetings, and I'm mortified to say that they might have gone door to door on more than one occasion to spread the word of the Lord Jesus. My brothers and I don't like to think about it too much.

Both of my brothers were older than me and I'll admit to having a charmed life through most of my childhood. I was the only girl, the youngest by more than ten years, and they all worshipped the ground I toddled on.

Robert was a doctor and my parents spent a great deal of time bragging about him to anyone who would listen. Jeremy had gone to law school and worked for the district attorney's office. My dad fancied him some modern-day crime solver—but then, Dad watched too much television.

Neither of my parents had come right out and said they were disappointed in me but it was pretty obvious that they didn't like the path my life had taken. The recent scandals around Tara and Sonya hadn't helped things either. My mother had taken to sending religious propaganda to my e-mail and dropping pamphlets off at my apartment when I wasn't home. At least, I sincerely hoped she was the one shoving them under my door or I'd have something else to worry about.

Both of my brothers were coming to dinner—Jeremy with

his too-perfect-to-live girlfriend and Robert had said he was bringing a "guest."

"Okay, you can do this." I turned off the ignition and sat back in the driver's seat. "You're a grown woman, with a job, a car payment, and an IRA account. You're totally in charge of your own life and you don't need their permission to do things that matter to you."

A gentle tap on my driver's-side window snapped me out of my pep talk and I screamed just a little. I turned to glare and found Jeremy standing beside my SUV with a big grin on his face. He opened my door for me and I slid out of the seat with a disgruntled sigh. "You suck."

"Hey, kiddo, you know I took a psych class in undergrad. I'm pretty sure that talking to yourself is a bad sign."

"If talking to myself was the worst of my problems I'd be just fine." I dropped my keys into my coat pocket and let him coax me up the sidewalk. "You love me, right?"

"Yep, more than my new golf clubs."

"I'll be your sister no matter what, right, Jer?"

He paused and frowned. "Have you killed someone? Because I didn't bring my truck and I don't want to put a body in the trunk of my new Lincoln. We'll have to take Rob's F150."

I laughed and relaxed. "No, I haven't killed someone."

"Okay, then," he said with a grin and wrapped his arm around me. "Sweetie, whatever your news is . . . you're my baby sister and nothing in the world could change that."

"Even if Mama gets really mad and cries?" I asked.

"Yeah, even then, and we both know she turns the waterworks on at the drop of the hat—so even if she cries you'll have to remember to keep your cool." He stopped at the door. "That bad, huh?"

"Could be."

"Can't be any worse than what Rob has up his sleeve. When

he found out you had something to tell us . . . he decided should put his cards on the table, too."

"Oh." I grinned. "He's brought Scott home to meet Mama and Daddy? Please, say it's true."

"It's true."

I sagged in relief. "That's awesome. My news isn't nearly as shocking as *that* is going to be."

Jeremy laughed. "It's bound to be an interesting evening. I warned Eva ahead of time that we might have to duck and cover. The good news is that Mama brought out the good dishes so maybe she won't throw them."

As it turned out, we made it all the way through dinner with my mother taking turns staring at me and Robert while Daddy talked golf and computers with Scott and Jeremy. The perfect girlfriend spent most of her time on her Blackberry texting everyone on the planet.

When it came time for dessert, my daddy dropped an amazingly large piece of cheesecake in front of me and then sat back in his chair.

"Come on, now. Can't be so bad that you're shaking." He patted my arm. "You know we love you, baby. So just say it."

"I'm twenty-nine years old." I took a deep breath and set down my fork. "And I don't know why I let myself get all worked up about this. I mean, I'm an adult. I pay taxes. I vote. I pay all of my own bills and . . ." I trailed off. "Shit."

"Kristen Marie!"

"Rose, let your daughter talk," my daddy interrupted with a sigh. "She is a grown woman, after all."

I grinned.

"Of course, Colin." My mother sat back in her chair and crossed her arms. Rose Davis was a beautiful woman; she must have been a real hottie in her day. I wondered if my father still saw that young girl when he looked at her. I had her face, her eyes, her wide, overgenerous mouth, but I had my father's dark hair.

"Four years ago, I started writing again. Mostly just for myself; like I did when I was younger." I picked up my fork and started to flake off pieces of the cheesecake. "Well, after I started working with the Marcus Group and I had a little extra cash I set myself up online and started publishing my work. It got a lot bigger than I ever thought it would and before I knew it, I had this big secret and I didn't know what to do with it."

"Are you in any kind of legal or financial trouble?" Jeremy asked quietly.

"No, of course not." I shook my head. "Far from it. I make good money selling my work myself—more than anyone thought I ever would just self-publishing. I never tried to submit my work to agents or publishers because it was just for me. Just for fun, really. In the beginning, I didn't charge much for the stories but then as the traffic on the site increased"—I took a deep breath—"I started putting out stories on a monthly basis and then I developed a section for members only and suddenly I had a thriving Internet business." I looked at my mother and she looked mostly confused. My daddy was decidedly amused and I figured he'd already gone down the road and deduced my destination.

"So, about three months ago I get an e-mail from an editor in New York. They want the rights to a series I've been writing online . . . print rights."

"That's cool." Eva offered me an encouraging smile. "I mean, that's what every author wants, right?"

"Yeah, it is," I admitted. "I mean, deep down I think all writers want their work to be read by as many people as possible. The thing is that I don't . . . well, I write erotica and I write under the name Lady Isabella."

Robert, the traitorous bastard, busted out laughing. Jeremy choked on his water and the color drained out of my mother's face.

"Kristen." My mother's eyes widened. "You're going to be on that show on Friday!"

Oh, boy. "Yes, Mama, I'm going to be on *Wake Up, Atlanta* on Friday."

"But . . . that Lady Isabella writes *porn*."

"No, Mama, I write erotica."

"Don't tell me that, young lady! I visited the Web site when they announced it yesterday because I was curious. There are half-naked people and *threesomes* in those books. I know you aren't writing that. I know it."

I rubbed the center of my forehead with two fingers and took a deep breath. "I grossed fifty thousand dollars last year as Lady Isabella and I signed a three-book deal with a publisher a week ago. I assure you: I do write it and that it is me."

My mother sputtered and then grew completely silent. It was unnerving so I turned to look at her to confirm she hadn't fainted or something equally dramatic and Southern.

"Mama?"

"Fifty thousand dollars, you say?" Rose took a deep breath. "Well, that's . . . lucrative."

Jeremy chuckled. "You don't say."

"But, it's porn, right?"

I groaned at my father's question. "Daddy!"

"Well, Kristen baby, it's okay if it's porn. You should be honest with yourself about what you're doing, that's all I'm saying."

"It's erotica." I bit down on my lip and wondered when we were going to get to the part where Robert hopped out of the closet. "Some of it is even romantic. It's not porn."

"Right," my father said dryly. "So if it's written for women . . . it's erotica."

"Right." I looked at Robert, who looked a little shocked and then Jeremy, who mostly looked amused. "Well?"

"Do you need help with the contracts? Did you get an agent to look things over?" Jeremy asked with a little grin. He was never going to let me live this down, I knew it.

"I have an agent." I looked toward Eva, who was texting avidly. "What are you doing, Eva?"

"Telling my best friend, Jenna, that I just met Lady Isabella." Eva grinned. "I'm not saying your real name or anything."

I bit down on my lip and tried to find a place to look in the room that wasn't occupied by a member of my family. My mother's dining room had never seemed smaller in my entire life. My parents were huddled on their end of the table having a hushed conversation that we could all hear perfectly well.

"Mother, it's not your fault!" I snapped. "And I'm not a pervert. I'm a perfectly normal, adult woman with a perfectly normal imagination. I don't need therapy and I didn't have any traumatic experiences as a child that you don't know about."

My mother huffed and then downed her entire glass of wine in one swallow. "How am I going to explain this to the ladies in my church group? Tell me that, young lady."

"You don't owe them an explanation about my behavior." I turned and glared at Robert. "Your turn."

Rob laughed. "Oh, no, baby sis. I'm not sure I could top this."

"Stop teasing her, Rob." Scott touched his arm. "And you promised."

He sighed. "Fine. Fine. But, I really don't think this is going to deflect from our baby sister, the Internet Porn Queen."

I threw my napkin at him, which was not the kind of table manners I'd been raised with, but it was either that or my fork.

He tossed the cloth napkin back to me and looked toward our parents with a sigh.

"Mama, Daddy: I'm gay. Scott and I aren't roommates, we're lovers. We decided to tell you now because we've decided to start a family and we found a surrogate to have a baby for us. She's due in six months."

"This is better than a movie," Eva whispered loudly to Jeremy in the overwhelming silence that followed.

"I told you, Colin," my mother said with a sigh. "Didn't I tell you? He hasn't brought a woman around to the house since he finished up his internship. I told you it wasn't normal for a grown man to have a roommate."

My daddy nodded. "Yes, ma'am, you did."

"A baby?" I asked with a grin. "Which one of you guys got to be the donor? Or is that a bad question to ask?"

"Scott is the donor and I'll be the donor on the next one. We'd like to have them about two years apart. The surrogate is a grad student and we purchased a donor egg as well so she has no biological attachment to the child," Robert explained. "Mama?"

"Well," my mother started and took that deep breath Southern women take when they've decided to rise above a situation and be a lady about things. "Will the two of you be getting married?"

"It's not legal in this state, Mama."

"Oh, well, I think a ceremony—a commitment ceremony sort of thing—wouldn't be out of place, even if had no legal standing."

My mouth dropped open. "Seriously?"

"Well, dear, I don't believe God puts limits on love as long as things are consensual and no harm is caused."

Jeremy choked again and, while Eva was slapping him on the back like she might have been a linebacker in a former life, I was left to ponder whether or not my mother had been taken over by an alien.

"Mama, you lectured me for two hours about my boss's sexual relationship!"

"I'm just worried about that poor girl. There is no telling what that man has talked her into doing. What with whips and chains and stuff," she explained patiently. "He's a pretty one, and Lord knows you can't trust a pretty man."

I figured in that moment that my mother had never said anything more truthful in her life. "Okay."

"Now, dear, are you sure you want to go on television and talk about this Lady Isabella business?"

"I don't want to do it at all but I don't have any choice in it." I sat back in my chair and abandoned was left of the cheesecake on my plate. "If I don't do it myself, someone is probably going to reveal who I am anyway. If I do it, it'll be less of a scandal, and the last thing the Marcus Group needs is another huge sex scandal."

Jeremy snorted. "Yeah, we sort of noticed."

I flushed. "Shut up."

"So what's up with that?" Eva asked. "You guys seem to be in the news a lot lately."

"We have a reporter stalking us around town, being a pain in the ass." And that was putting it lightly as far as I was concerned. Now that I was in Jean's cross hairs I felt exposed and violated. I had no idea how I was going to feel when she finally let loose on me. "I don't even know if this is what she's going to focus on next. All I do know is that she has it in for us and I'm the only one she hasn't picked on yet."

"Maybe she can't find any gossip on you," Eva consoled. "You are kind of boring despite this new thing. I mean, no one would ever think in a million years that you were Lady Isabella."

I knew she was trying to be comforting but all I wanted to

do was jump over the table and stab her in the head with my dessert fork. Thank God I hadn't wasted it on Robert.

"Eva's right, sweetie. When is the last time you even had a date?" My mother smiled softly when I looked her way and I wondered if she realized she had the devil in her.

All the way home, I turned the conversation over in my head. From my confession, to my brother admitting he was gay and that there was a grad student somewhere in the city having his gay lover's baby, and I really couldn't figure out how the entire thing had boiled down to a question about my recent dating activities and lack of a love life.

Once in my apartment, I went online and changed my bio with a few decisive clicks of my mouse. Then I sent Adam an e-mail with a link to my Web site and an invitation for dinner on Saturday. The whole thing was a disaster waiting to happen but I was proud of myself for following through with my plan.

3

An hour later, my doorbell rang and I forced myself off the couch to answer it. I threw the door open and glared at Adam for a few seconds. "I'm not boring."

He grinned and glanced me over. "Not even a little bit."

"I'm a grown woman with a good career and a thriving personal business."

"And a fantastic ass." Adam grinned and slipped past me into my apartment. "Very intelligent and creative. Great legs."

"What are you doing here? It's not Saturday."

"Yeah, about that." He turned around and put his hands on his hips. "Did you make the date for Saturday so the scandal of this Lady Isabella thing would be in full swing and I would beg off or something? Because, honestly, if you think that shit is going to scare either one of us off, you're crazy."

"It might have crossed my mind," I admitted softly and then sighed. "You can't . . . don't you see how stupid it would be to get involved with me? I mean, the rumors about you and Neal are mostly handled at this point, right? It died down pretty quickly when everyone realized those pictures were from a funeral. Now, if you've seen out in public with a woman who writes porn and specializes in *threesomes* . . . what kind of impression is that going to make?"

Adam grinned then. "Well, you're gorgeous and he's just as fine, so I guess people would think I was a very lucky bastard."

I huffed. "Shut up. We live in Georgia, for the love of God. You play a professional sport in the Bible Belt! Do you have any idea what the religious nutjobs in this area are going to say about me when this comes out? My own mother thinks I must be hiding some childhood trauma that she doesn't know about. She took my brother—her baby boy—coming out of the closet better than she did my little news."

Adam snorted. "Your brother is gay?"

"Yeah." I dropped down onto my couch. "Apparently my mother had suspected as much the entire time . . . and I was really hoping that she'd throw a big ol' tantrum about his being gay and overlook my little thing."

Adam sat down beside me and laughed softly. "Not very nice of you."

"Yeah, well, all's fair in love and war, right? And you haven't seen war until you've disappointed a Southern woman over the age of fifty. I fully expect her to show up with her church group and try to do an intervention and maybe—God help me—an exorcism."

"Is she Catholic?"

"No, but it won't stop her from dragging some poor priest off the street and convincing him he needs to save her only daughter from a life of sin."

Adam plucked up one of my hands. "Was it really that bad?"

"Well, the amount of money I made last year did make her pause and consider her words more carefully." I jerked a little when my doorbell rang again. "Reinforcements?"

Adam chuckled. "I sent him the link and told him I was coming over here." He stood up from the couch and walked to the door. "I thought it best that we not arrive at the same time."

I sighed heavily and wondered if it would be okay if I opened the bottle of wine that Tara had bought me for Christmas the year before. If ever I needed to get really drunk, tonight was the night. I turned and watched Neal slide into the apartment and shrug out of his jacket. I was in way over my head and there was no end in sight.

"Hey, I take it you've had a pretty stressful day." Neal dropped into a chair across from me and raised an eyebrow in question. "Lady Isabella?"

"Yeah." I huffed out a breath. "Crazy, huh?"

"Pretty hot, actually," Neal admitted. "Why are you 'coming out,' so to speak?"

"I'm probably going to be outed by that crazy-ass journalist who makes it her business to tear Tara and Sonya down in the press. I can't help but think I'll be next, and Lady Isabella is my biggest secret." At least, I thought, it was my biggest secret a week ago. I had a feeling as I watched them get comfortable in my living room that my biggest secret was about to get life sized.

"So, did you think we weren't going to be interested in coming over to play after your interview on Friday?" Neal asked, one dark eyebrow raising in amusement.

"It crossed my mind. Neither one of you needs this kind of publicity, and if I'm seen with one of you in public . . . well, conclusions could be drawn."

Adam laughed. "Yes, they could. I'm drawing conclusions as I sit here." He plucked up one of my hands and rubbed it between his own large ones. "Your hands are freezing. We don't make you nervous, do we?"

"No, not at all." I was stunned to realize how much I meant that. There had been a time in my life when the kind of attention I was getting from both of them would have been overwhelming. But being the center of their attention wasn't more than I could handle, which was a relief considering where I saw the situation headed.

"Good." Adam released my hand and relaxed on the couch. "So, this woman who is out to make your lives hell—is there anything you can do about her?"

"Well." I frowned as I started and then stood so I could move around. "Sonya was all about kicking her ass but Tara vetoed violence in favor of stoic Southern femaleness. Apparently, we are to consider Jean Turst something like the marching Union army, which is to say we should endure her petty little ways, consider ourselves above the situation, and just hope like hell she doesn't burn down our houses on her way out of town." I paced toward the kitchen. "Wine?" I didn't wait for a response because I figured they were both too polite to let me drink alone.

"Have you considered a lawyer?" Neal asked as he watched me move around the open kitchen. "I mean, if she's practically stalking the three of you . . ."

"Well, it's her job, right? I mean, we can't find any kind of legal fault with her activities and she hasn't exactly outright lied about anything. She's just embellished and preyed on a couple of situations that were just ripe for the picking." The doorbell rang and I groaned.

Setting aside the unopened wine, I rubbed my hands on my skirt and glanced at my guests. I really didn't want to have to tell them to hide and was relieved when they both stood and moved out of view of the door. A quick look out the peep-hole made my eyes cross in irritation and my stomach tighten. I leaned briefly against the door and then jerked when Jean Turst used her fist to bang on the door.

I flipped the security bar into place so she couldn't push her way in and opened the door enough that we could see each other. "What are you doing here, Jean?"

"I thought we should talk. I'd like to make a deal with you."

"A deal with me?" I asked and then laughed. "On what?"

"You should let me come in so we can discuss this like adults."

"No. It's bad enough that I have to deal with you at work; I'm not going to let you taint where I have to sleep as well." I shot a glare over my shoulder when Adam snickered. "What do you want, Jean?"

"Lady Isabella."

I sighed. "Yes, that's my pen name. It's not exactly a state secret. What about it?"

"I want Lady Isabella."

I stared and frowned my confusion. "I don't understand."

"The money. I want the money you've earned stealing my dream."

I'd never even taken a basic psychology class in college but I was pretty convinced I was dealing with a crazy woman. "Jean, you've got me at a loss. I have no idea what you're talking about."

"You weren't even serious about writing in college. It was just something you did to pass the time; it was never something you meant to make a career. You said it over and over again that it was just a hobby for you."

"And it is. My writing and my Web site are a hobby—a way I spend my free time that is relaxing and rewarding. That's what a hobby is, Jean."

"Two hundred thousand dollars should cover it. That's what I want from you." She pressed her hand to keep the door open. "It's the least of what you owe me."

"And if I don't? If I refuse to do what you want?"

"I'm going to release another story and I'll keep finding stories until I run your friend out of business. I'm going to tell the world you make your living writing porn on the side. Don't think I won't."

"As I said, Jean, my hobby isn't a state secret." I sighed. "I signed a contract with a publisher a week ago for print rights, and the bio on the Lady Isabella Web site lists my real name and picture. I'm going to be interviewed by *Wake Up, Atlanta* on Friday."

I watched her face go pale and then color rushed back across her cheeks as she pressed her lips together. She was so crazy and more than a little pathetic. I was really glad I'd put the security bar into place before I opened the door.

"You think that solves everything?"

"I think that if you don't leave Tara Marcus alone, her daddy is going to buy the newspaper you work for and have you fired." I responded with a sigh. "Jean, you need to take a step back and evaluate the entire situation. I don't know . . . I really don't have the first clue what is going on in your life or why after all of these years you feel the need to make things so horrible for us but it's going to get you nowhere fast. You just tried to blackmail me, for fuck's sake. Look, go get laid or something. And, seriously, stop watching TV movies. Real people don't act like this."

"You're going to regret all of this."

"Sure, sure, just keep going. Find something on me; the more scandal surrounding Lady Isabella the better my book sales will be." I leaned on the door. "Maybe you could write a story about the threesome I had with the two hot aliens who captured me for breeding purposes." I wiggled my eyebrows and she huffed out a breath of annoyance. "Or maybe, about the two brothers who rescued me in the Old West and took me home to keep. Isolated mountain cabin, two men who are so lonely they are willing to share a wife ..." I grinned. "Nah, probably not, because that's all fiction."

"This isn't funny."

"It really isn't." I responded and then frowned at her. "Stop playing games, Jean, and go away. I don't know what we did to you in college to make you hate us so much but if you don't get over yourself and over it, you're going to start to make enemies you can't handle. I wasn't kidding about Tara's father. He's kept his nose out of this situation so far but if you start to make it difficult for his baby girl to make a living, he's going to get fed up and put his big, rich foot down."

"This isn't over."

"Of course not, sweetie, it never is with crazy people." I moved to shut the door and frowned at her when she pressed against it to try to keep it open. "Go away, Jean, before I call the police and file charges against you for attempting to black-mail me."

"You'd need proof. It would be your word against mine."

I laughed then. "I'm not alone, Jean." A large hand slid down my back and Adam moved into her view as he tucked me close. "It'll be our word against yours."

Jean glared at him and then turned to me. "And here I was thinking you were the only one who wasn't fucking a client."

"Not yet, but it's certainly on the agenda," Adam told her cheerfully. He put his own hand over mine on the door and shut the door firmly.

Torn between laughing at the absurdity of the situation and crying in sheer frustration, I turned the bolt on the door and slid away from him to walk toward the kitchen. "Now, where was I?"

"About to drown your sorrows in a bottle of wine," Neal told me with a little grin. He handed me a glass and looked me over with a frown. "How big of a threat is this woman?"

"That depends on how truly crazy she is," I responded and then reached for my phone. I dialed Tara's number more from muscle memory than anything else, because my brain was basically numb. I winced when Joshua answered. "Hey, Josh, I need to talk to Tara if she's not tied up." Neal and Adam laughed softly but I glared at them and blushed. "I, uh, didn't mean it the way that sounded."

Joshua Keller laughed in my ear. "She's actually in the kitchen. We normally save rope play for weekends."

"Oh." My cheeks got a little warmer as I waited and then I sighed when she came on the line. "Jean Turst just tried to blackmail me for two hundred thousand dollars."

Tara was silent for a long moment and I could almost see her trying her calming exercises, her eyes shut and her lips moving slightly while she counted to a thousand in prime numbers. She wasn't very good at the prime number thing and always got pissed off. It sort of split her temper between outside stimuli and internal failure—so while it not might work the way it was intended, it did help her focus.

"Okay, and you told her to fuck off?"

"I told her she was crazy. She threatened to out me over the Lady Isabella thing if I didn't pay her. Said I *owed* her for stealing her dream, whatever the fuck that means. I really think she's a few bricks shy."

"She's more than a few bricks shy of a full load," Tara returned evenly. "Okay, that's enough. I'm going to call my daddy."

I sagged a little in relief. I'd pretty much wanted her to sic her daddy on Jean Turst since the whole thing had started. "Thanks. Tell him I said hi."

"I'm also calling our lawyer to see about some restraining orders. That's twice she's contacted you and I think considering the content of her last conversation we could probably get the court to order her to stay away from you for a while."

"Well, this time she showed up at my apartment and I have a witness . . . or two." I blushed as I looked toward Adam and Neal. They were on the couch watching the television with closed captions. It said a lot about my life that the thing had already been on ESPN when they turned it on. "Tara?"

"Two?" She asked amused. "Jesus, don't keep me in suspense."

"I think you know which two," I snapped.

She laughed, that beautiful laugh she does when she's really pleased and can't stop herself. "Oh, dear. Wow. That's the hottest thing I've ever pictured in my life."

"Well, stop picturing it." I ran my fingers through my hair and then hissed when I got caught up in the clip I was still wearing. I wrenched my fingers free and then unclipped the metal torture device. "Seriously. Stop picturing me naked."

"Sure, okay, give me an hour and I'm sure I'll get it out of my head," Tara chuckled again. "Wow. Just wow. I thought you were going to set up a date with Adam this weekend."

"It's not a date. It's a . . ." I waved my hand and then glared at them when they both smirked at me. "It's . . . do you think that this thing with Jean is going to be over once your daddy starts buying things and firing people?"

She laughed at the abrupt change of subject. "Well, it's obvious she has an agenda and her ploy to take money from you is telling. She's never contacted me or asked me directly for money but we both know she has the best chance of getting money out of the Marcus name." Tara took a deep breath. "I think she picked on you and Sonya both in an effort to get my attention. I mean she started with me when she provoked the situation with Joshua and the Playground. It's been leading somewhere and if the road isn't to money, then where would it go?"

"I don't know. This nonsense about me stealing her dream is a little extreme." I left my wineglass on the counter and walked across the room to the large window that displayed most of my living room and a great view of the city. I pulled the blinds shut with a snap and wondered if Jean had already taken a few pictures. "This can't possibly be about that guy in college or even my writing career."

"What guy in college?" Neal asked Adam in a loud whisper. I turned to watch Adam shrug off the question.

"And really, she is a professional journalist. I can't see how my hobby could really be a problem for her."

"Your little hobby just got you a book deal," Tara reminded gently. "And a side income that could fairly soon rival what you make with me."

"It's not something . . . I really like my job with you, Tara. I have no intention of leaving unless you think I should. I mean, if you think Jean would leave you alone if I was no longer at the Marcus Group . . ."

"No, and shut up. I'm not going to let that twit run you off. Like I said, if it really boils down to money, then it's probably been about me the entire time. You aren't the one with the trust fund and a filthy-rich daddy." Tara sighed. "Look, forget about this stuff for a while. Take tomorrow off so you can prep for Friday and then shut yourself in for the weekend to regroup. We don't have many deep dark secrets left for her to exploit and I'm sure my father is just waiting to pounce. I'll call him tonight."

"Yeah, okay." I disconnected the phone call and tossed my phone onto a chair near the window. "She's going to activate the *Damsel in Distress* signal and her Daddy is going to ride to the rescue."

"She doesn't strike me as the kind to run to her father."

I snorted before I could help myself. Rubbing my nose in horror, I shrugged off the rude behavior and went after my wine-glass. "We all have our breaking point and now Turst has put her cards out on the table. She wants money."

They let me finish off my wine in silence and then Neal re-filled my glass with a little smile. "Relax, little one, we aren't trying to get you drunk so we can do filthy things to you. We'd rather you be sober for the main event."

I took note that he'd only given me half a glass, and then glanced toward my phone when it started to ring again. I went and dug it out of the chair I'd thrown it on and flipped it on after I checked the caller ID. It was not exactly who I expected. "Hello."

"Kristen, my Tara tells me you're a soon to be very famous writer and that Jean Turst woman is trying to blackmail you."

"Huh, well, Mr. Marcus . . . it's . . . she told me she wanted two hundred thousand dollars or she was going to publish a story about how I sell porn on the Internet." I dropped down in the chair and tucked the phone against my shoulder. "But I assume that Tara told you about my television appearance on Friday?"

"Yes." Andrew Marcus chuckled in my ear. His daughter had inherited his rich, unencumbered laugh. "I look forward to it. I plan to tell everyone I know about you. It's quite interest-ing. I visited your Web site while I was talking to my girl. You did decline to pay the woman, correct?"

"I work for my money, Mr. Marcus, I'm certainly not going to part with it for such a stupid thing. I'm going to be outing myself on Friday anyway and she can print whatever she wants in the newspaper."

"Tara tells me you stole her boyfriend in college."

"Oh, I did not!" I blushed and bit down on my bottom lip. "I didn't, Mr. Marcus. He was just interested in me and dumped her to ask me out."

"Call me Andrew, young lady. I've dated women younger than you."

I sniffed. "I noticed. It's my personal policy not to call womanizers by their first name." I could almost hear his grin through the phone. "But, I suppose I could make an exception in your case. What do you need from me?"

"Nothing. I just wanted to check on my girl and make sure you didn't need anything. Should I send over some personal security? I have a few on staff who are lounging around looking bored."

My mouth dropped open. "No, sir, I don't need a security team."

"Are you sure? I could send you a couple of big strapping ex-Marines. I'll make sure to send pretty ones," Andrew offered with an unrepentant laugh.

"Oh, you're horrible." I seriously doubted that my face could get any hotter at that point and I pointedly looked away from Neal and Adam, who were looking at me with shrewd, knowing eyes. "I don't need you to send over any ex-Marines either. I've got company."

"Really? Who, should I have their background checked?"

"Did you do a background check on Joshua Keller?"

"Absolutely, sweetheart. You don't think I'd let a man who likes to tie up women and spank them date my daughter if I hadn't had him thoroughly investigated, do you?" Andrew laughed again.

"I'll be fine. Thanks for being rich and throwing your money around. It's appreciated."

"You're welcome. Have Tara call me immediately if this woman shows up again."

After I promised—though I was sort of hoping that Jean would go away or at least find someone new to pick on—he let me get off the phone and then I only had the two men lounging on my couch to deal with. They were both staring at me intently, and suddenly I felt a lot like prey.

"You know, normally I make a man take me out for several weeks before he even gets into my apartment. At least five dates."

Neal and Adam shared a look and Neal sighed. "We could split the dates. I'll handle all of the ridiculous stuff like museums, art galleries, and concerts."

Adam nodded. "I'll take the semi-fun stuff like hiking, picnics, skate parks, and crap like that."

I laughed at them and they both grinned. "You're both utter assholes. But you know that, right?"

"Yeah." Adam slid over a little and then patted the couch between them. "It's something you'll have to get used to."

"You two do this often?"

Neal smiled and took a sip of his wine. "What would you say if I told you we prefer it?"

"Prefer it?" I bit down on my lip. "You prefer to share a woman?"

"Yes," Adam said and then patted the couch again. "Come here, Kristen."

I was in so much trouble and wasn't that an extremely thrilling thought. Standing, I walked to the couch and stood there between them. "So that little show in the office today?"

"Would you have preferred we just say it for everyone to hear?" Neal asked amused. "It's a good way to gauge the court . . . pick out who is willing to play our game and who isn't."

"And the girl in Vegas?"

"Was the same girl we've been hooking up with on and off since college," Adam explained as I slid onto the couch with them. "Though honestly, none of us have very solid memories of that night."

"Speak for yourself," I muttered into my wineglass and then raised an eyebrow at Neal. "I think Neal has a memory or two."

Neal smirked. "Nothing concrete."

Yeah, right. But, I figured that was an argument best left for the two of them, if they ever intended on having it. I think, really, that Neal liked knowing and Adam liked speculating about what happened. I certainly liked speculating about what happened and I hadn't even been there.

"So, all those times you asked me out?" I looked at Adam and frowned slightly. "What was the plan?"

"A few dates, then maybe dinner over at my house with Neal in tow . . ." Adam grinned and didn't look the least bit guilty. "Then one night I'd have an emergency and Neal would show up to have dinner with you instead so you wouldn't get stood up."

"So, I'd end up dating you both and not even know it." I laughed and shook my head. "Then you would spring the trap."

"Something like that, but you make it sound very . . . sordid." Neal relaxed on the couch and sighed. "It's really not."

"It really is but that's okay because I like sordid. You guys ever strike out with a girl before?"

"Yeah, a few years back there was a girl who I started dating." Neal chuckled. "She never caught on to our game but she did make several pointed attempts to make me choose between her and Adam. There were a lot of comments about three being a crowd."

"I'm pretty sure three is a party," Adam said as he took my empty glass from my hand and set it aside. "Four is an event and five is orgy."

"Five for an orgy?" Neal asked and frowned a little.

"Five or more," Adam conceded.

Neal agreed with a little tilt of his head and then put aside his own glass. "Should we leave, little one? We've given you a lot of food for thought."

Did I want them to leave? I didn't know what I wanted exactly but after the night I had I figured I deserved something fun and hot. Something they were both interested in giving me. I sighed and let my head fall back onto the couch. There was no way in hell I could ask for what I wanted and I wondered when they were going to realize it. They were way out of my league and I was in over my head and any other cliché I could think of.

"Three's a party, huh?"

"Yep," Adam winked when I glanced his way.

"I don't understand how this is going to work."

"Mechanics or public perception?" Neal asked as he moved a little closer to me. "Because I was pretty sure you understood the mechanics."

I laughed. "Yeah, okay, I get the mechanics. Granted, that required some Internet research in the beginning and I might have watched more porn than a woman should admit to watching but . . . yeah, I understand the mechanics."

"Did you keep the porn?"

I blushed and they both laughed. "I plead the Fifth."

"We'll find out eventually," Adam promised. "Most of the time, if we have a long-term lover in our lives, the public relationship is with me because Neal has a reputation for being a player. It works out because people expect him to play around and hang out with me. No one questions it."

I frowned. "So, he fucks around a lot?"

"No." Adam ran fingers along my jaw and rubbed my bottom lip with his thumb. "But, that is the public perception. It works in our favor and keeps people from wondering if there is more going on than what is on the surface."

"But, if you go out with me, people might suspect differently. I mean, my writing career and the picture of you two that were published earlier in the week." I took a deep breath. "It's a big risk."

"People aren't going to look at us and automatically think that you spend your nights tucked up between the two of us.

No one really understands or even expects to see a polyamorous relationship. Since they won't look for it, even with your writing career exposed, they aren't going to see it. I honestly think someone would have to catch the three of us in bed to really draw that conclusion."

I knew two women who would jump all over that conclusion without even blinking but that was beside the point.

"Yeah, at most they'll think you're his beard," Neal chuckled as he said it. "Wow, who knew he'd need one?"

"Shut up," Adam muttered. "Asshole."

I blinked briefly at the word and asked a question I never thought in a million years I would ask a man, much less two. "Is double penetration on the menu?" They both jerked and looked at me. "What?" I nodded my head toward Adam but focused on Neal. "He said I could have whatever I want. That the two of you would do whatever I needed."

Neal cleared his throat and then chuckled. "Well, aren't you a surprise?" He leaned forward and brushed his mouth against mine. "Is that what you want, little one?"

"If it is?" I asked, wetting my bottom lip with a frown. "If that's what I want . . . is that okay?"

"Yeah," Adam murmured as he stood. "That is okay." He offered me his hand and I took it with the best smile I could offer.

I wondered if insanity ran in my family. That would have explained so much about my mother.

4

They moved together like they'd been doing this for years and I wasn't even really concerned by that. Nimble fingers made quick work of my dress and all the undergarments I'd layered underneath it until I stood stark naked between two fully clothed men. It was exciting and arousing in a way I'd never known before.

"Anything off the table?" Neal asked against my throat as he slid one large hand down my back and over my ass. His fingers dipped briefly between my cheeks and brushed against my anus deliberately.

"I don't have a lot of experience with this but I'm willing to try anything at least once. Condoms are a must."

Adam chuckled and kissed my mouth gently as he rubbed my stomach in a small circle. It made me absurdly thankful that Tara dragged me to the gym four times a week. "Good. Beyond what you've already asked for"—he took a deep breath—"Is there anything else you want?"

"Just your attention," I admitted with a blush. "I really

wouldn't consider myself submissive or anything like that but I don't want to be in charge. I'm tired of making decisions."

"You'll give your pleasure over to us?" Neal asked, his teeth catching briefly on my earlobe. "Do you understand what that means?"

"Yes, that would be perfect. I understand."

"Good." Adam kissed me again. "Get on the bed."

I pulled the comforter and top sheet off the bed and dropped them both onto the floor before I crawled up into the middle and knelt there. They both offered me a smirk when they realized I was intent on watching them undress. Neal inspected my face for a few seconds and then with a little quirk of his lips reached out and started unbuttoning Adam's shirt. Adam chuckled softly and then glanced my way before he surrendered himself to being undressed by his friend.

I shifted happily on my knees and tried to ignore the way my nipples were starting to get hard and tight. Never once had I thought that I was the kind of woman who would be aroused just by watching others. In college, I'd had a roommate who made it her goal in life to fuck her boyfriend when she *knew* I was awake and could listen. I'd never gotten aroused by the display but she'd certainly gotten off knowing I was awake to listen.

Neal tossed Adam's shirt and then his T-shirt onto a chair and then ran one hand down Adam's chest, his fingers skating over the muscled ridges of Adam's abs as he reached for his belt. "You okay?"

Adam nodded and then grinned. "More than."

Neal smirked and unfastened the belt slowly. I wondered if Adam felt half as teased as I did. I looked at his face and found him watching his best friend intently without the slightest sign of discomfort. Neal pulled the belt free slowly and then considered it for a second. "If your little friend Tara was here, we'd probably want to keep track of this."

I laughed and then blushed. "I don't know if I'd like that kind of thing."

"No," Adam murmured. "You aren't the type. Maybe candle wax or sensual biting, but not anything like a belt. If you like pain at all, it would be on the softer side of things."

Sensual biting. Jesus. I had to admit the thought of a man biting me had me a little more excited than normal. I shifted a little as Neal dropped the belt and unfastened Adam's jeans. I could tell by the way they drifted closer together that this little display was turning them both on. Adam toed off his shoes and then sucked in a breath as Neal stripped him of his pants and his boxers in a move that was far too practiced.

"I think he's had a bit of experience at undressing men." I grinned when Adam looked my way.

"Yeah," Adam agreed, his gaze drifting over my hard-tipped breasts and then traveling downward briefly to the apex of my thighs before settling on my face. "We're going to have a lot of fun, sweetheart."

"I sincerely hope so." I grinned when Neal laughed.

Neal toed off his own shoes and started to pull his shirt free from his pants when Adam stopped him. "Let me."

"Jesus." Neal took a deep breath as he dropped his hands to his sides. "You don't have to."

"I want to," Adam murmured and stepped closer. His hard and already leaking cock brushed against Neal's hand as they got closer. Both hissed in a breath but neither backed away.

Adam wasn't as smooth as Neal's, but his nervousness was sexy and just as rewarding as Neal's elegant and knowing process had been. He pulled the shirt free of Neal's slacks and then over his head with a little assistance and tossed it on top of the pile of clothes Neal had already made in the chair. His fingers trembled slightly as he reached for Neal's belt but he steadied them quickly and unbuckled him with confidence.

"You like this," Neal murmured.

"Yes," Adam and I both answered at the same time. They both looked my way and a small smile flitted across Adam's generous mouth.

Neal laughed and then took a deep breath when Adam pulled the belt free and dropped it onto the floor. "Don't bite off more than you can chew, buddy."

"You've got nothing I can't handle, pal," Adam muttered in return. He caught the tab of Neal's zipper and eased it down carefully. "You like this, too."

"I really do," Neal admitted without a single hesitation.

Adam wet his bottom lip as he let Neal's slacks drop away and pool at his feet. Adam's fingers danced along the top of the waistband of his fitted boxers and he grinned when Neal took a deep, unsteady breath. "What should we do first?"

Neal groaned a little as Adam hooked his fingers into the sides of his boxers and pulled them down as he went to his knees. "Jesus, Adam."

"Flattering, but no." Adam jerked his head in my direction. "She's such a little voyeur."

"She really is."

"I *really* am," I said with a sigh and then watched, amused, as Adam got rid of Neal's socks and then his own. "Will you touch him?"

"Is that what you want?" Adam asked, his voice a little hoarse and uncertain.

"Not if it makes you uncomfortable." I watched as Adam, still on his knees, ran his fingers up Neal's legs and then over his thighs. "Oh."

Neal reached out and with a shaking hand ran his fingers

through Adam's hair. "I thought we weren't going to let her make any decisions."

Adam stood and turned to stare at me. "That's right. So what should we do first?"

"Well, obviously, she must be taught her place." Neal regarded me with shrewd dark eyes and I couldn't help but smile. "Yes, she must be taught a lesson."

"Lay down on your back," Adam said as he walked to stand by the bed, Neal followed along silently. "Spread your legs."

Neal moved down to the end of the bed and then licked his bottom lip as he crawled onto the bed between my spread thighs. "Tell him where you keep your condoms and lubrication."

I flushed, because I kept those items in a drawer right beside my collection of vibrators, including my most recent purchase. Something I hadn't even gotten the courage to use yet. I bit down on my lip as Neal ran his hands along my thighs, touching me in much the same way Adam had touched him and then hooked them both under my knees to spread my legs wider.

"Bottom drawer on the right." I motioned toward my dresser and hoped that a woman couldn't literally die of mortification right in the middle of a threesome.

I was obviously hiding nothing from Neal because the moment Adam opened the drawer he spoke. "Bring anything fun she might have as well."

Adam laughed. "Not a problem." He tilted his head and looked at me. "Anything in this drawer that you'd prefer stay in it?"

They both paused, and I realized this was probably the last question I'd get asked. "No, I'm good with everything in there."

"Very interesting collection," Adam murmured and then pulled out a box of unopened condoms and a bottle of lube that was mostly full. He brought those back to the bed and then returned to the drawer. I wasn't surprised when he returned opening the packaging of the butt plug. He dropped the box and plastic in a trash can and then quirked an eyebrow at Neal. "I'm going to wash this, just in case. Be right back."

"Yeah," Neal agreed.

"Do carry on," Adam called over his shoulder and I laughed softly as Neal returned his attention to me.

"Thank you."

"For what?" Neal whispered.

"Making this fun and not awkward."

"Sex should be fun," he responded as he lowered his head and placed a soft kiss on my inner thigh. "And dirty."

"Yeah," I agreed, shifting under his hands and then biting down on my bottom lip. He'd barely even kissed me and he was closer to my pussy than the last two men I'd dated had ever gotten.

"And intimate." He brushed a kiss over my belly button and then he drifted upward to capture one nipple briefly. He sucked hard and gave me the hint of teeth before he lifted away and sought my mouth with single-minded determination.

I groaned into his kiss, relieved that he'd understood my unvoiced need. His strong, heavy body settled on top of mine and I shifted under him, my thighs clenching against his hips. His thick, heavy cock pressed hard against my stomach, leaving a trail of pre-cum that made me shiver. Neal surged against me briefly and I met the thrust of his body in answer and he groaned into my mouth.

The mattress dipped and he lifted his mouth from mine as Adam lay down beside us. Neal moved to my other side and they both stared at me for a few long seconds and then Adam sighed.

"It's like my birthday and Christmas," Adam murmured.

Neal laughed. "Yeah, it sure is." His fingers danced over my stomach, catching and playing with the trail of pre-cum he'd left on my skin. "So soft and beautiful. Innocent. All of our filthy plans seem almost a sacrilege at this point."

I forced myself to remain still as Adam's fingers joined Neal's in exploring my stomach before they both drifted upward and rubbed the wetness they'd both found over my nipples. "Oh."

Neal lowered his head and sucked my damp nipple into his mouth and I arched up off the bed in surprise. Adam followed suit seconds later and all I could think was that they were both sucking Neal's pre-cum off of me. It was dirty—almost nasty—and I loved it. Their hands drifted over my stomach and mingled together as they converged between my legs. Fingers danced over my labia, teasing my clit while others teased at my hole and one large finger slid into my pussy.

Neal lifted his head and met my gaze. "Been a while?"

"Yes." I swallowed hard. "Is that a problem?"

"Not at all." He lowered his head and kissed my mouth with a brush of his lips. "We're going to turn you over and put the plug in. Have you ever taken a man that way?"

"Just once."

"Did you enjoy it?"

"A little but . . . he wasn't very comfortable, so . . . you know."

"Yeah, I know." His gaze locked with mine. "The plug will help you stretch out and get used to the penetration. We're both going to fuck you while it's in place and then . . . we're going to fuck you at the same time." He chuckled as I gasped. "Right now, Adam is going to lick your pretty little clit until you come for us. It'll get you all relaxed so we can work on the plug."

"Okay." I swallowed hard as Adam abandoned my nipple and slid down my body with practiced ease. He shouldered his way between my legs and slid his big hands under my ass as Neal pulled his fingers free of my clenching pussy. "Fuck."

209

It had been years since a man had put his mouth on me. The last lover I had thought it was disgusting. He hadn't lasted long as a result of that rude admission. Adam nuzzled against my labia and then his tongue darted out to brush against my throbbing clit. I melted into the bed and tucked my face against Neal's shoulder as Adam started to suck and lick my clit.

"He loves this," Neal murmured. "He's been talking about eating your sweet little pussy since we set eyes on you." He tapped my lips with the two fingers he'd had inside me and I sucked them into my mouth without a single pause. "Do you like to lick and suck, too?"

I could only nod as he used his fingers to fuck my mouth. The taste of his skin combined with the taste of my own juices was startling and I loved it. He pulled them away before I was remotely ready and then moved to his knees. Before I could protest, he pressed his cock against my lips and I sucked the head of him in without a whimper of complaint.

Neal worked his cock in and out of my mouth carefully, never pushing in deep enough to hurt me but controlling everything about the act. His fingers trailed through my hair and I moaned around his cock as Adam coaxed an orgasm from me. I scrambled against the bed as he dipped his tongue into me and lapped at the juices that were flowing out of me.

"Shhh . . . just relax," Neal murmured, his hand stilling me. He pulled his cock from my mouth and laughed softly when I frowned. "Trust me, sweetheart, this is just the beginning."

They maneuvered me onto my knees and I briefly buried my face against the mattress. I couldn't even believe I was on my bed with my ass in the air, but I'd asked for this and they were certainly going to give it to me. Fingers drifted through my hair as they moved around on the bed and I lifted my head to find Adam with me at the top of the bed. Which meant the large hands rubbing my lower back were Neal's. Adam shifted so he was resting against a few pillows at the head of the bed and spread his legs out on either side of me.

"Suck me, Kris."

It was a distraction, I knew that, but I could hardly turn down having a cock in my mouth. The first time I'd given a man a blow job lived in my memory vividly. Not just because I'd been clumsy and a little dangerous with my teeth but because as inexperienced as I was, his pleasure had been mine to give. The power of that had made me eager for it and maybe that eagerness had made up for the fact that I hadn't had a clue what I was doing.

Adam's cock lay full and hard against his stomach, a little longer than Neal's but not as thick. I ran my tongue up the length of him, ignoring his squirming and his hands that had come to rest on my shoulders as I teased the head of him with my tongue. After a few swipes, I tucked him in and started to suck in earnest, letting him slide deep into the recesses of my mouth with each downward stroke. I was so intent on the cock gliding into my mouth that the first hot, wet swipe of Neal's tongue across my anus was so shocking that I choked a little.

Adam pulled free of my mouth and soothed me with gentle hands and soft words. I let my forehead rest against his hip and rocked gently as I worked my way through a series of emotions ranging from horror to amazement. I'd never once in my entire life had a man put his mouth on me the way Neal was and the fact that I was enjoying it so much had me shaken.

His tongue slid into me and a sound halfway between a protest and a sob escaped my mouth. It was probably the nastiest thing a man had ever done to me and I was excited beyond words. I wondered what other kinky little things were lurking in my brain just waiting to get out.

Adam guided me back to his cock and I gratefully concentrated on sucking him off. The last thing I really needed was an in-depth analysis of why I enjoyed getting rimmed. I was both grateful and disappointed when he stopped but tried to keep both reactions to myself.

Adam threaded his fingers into my hair and lifted me off his cock with a little sigh of regret. "Okay, sweetheart, I don't want you taking a bite out of me with another surprise."

I grinned. "No, that wouldn't be a good idea."

"Neal is going to put a single finger inside you so he can start stretching you out for the plug. The plug isn't as large as a dick but it'll give you a nice full feeling for when we fuck you." He ran his thumb over my bottom lip as a cool slick finger breached my ass.

Neal patted my hip with his free hand. "Just take a deep breath for me, and relax. You've done this before, right?"

"Yeah, once or twice."

I shivered when he added a second finger and slowly started to fuck in and out of me with the kind of skill I certainly wasn't going to question. I pressed a kiss against Adam's hand and then lowered my head until I could take him back into my mouth. He accepted the attention with a little sigh and it became my life goal to get him off. They were both intent on working me up until I was stupid with it, and it was time I got some of my own back.

His hips jerked under my hands and he groaned as I started to bob up and down on him intently. I used each upward stroke to press my tongue against the back of his cock before swirling it around the head to savor the fluid he was leaking for me. Neal's fingers abandoned me and I slowed down slightly so I wouldn't hurt either one of us when he placed the plug.

The steady pressure of the plastic butt plug was different than his fingers and it pressed so much deeper. He smacked my ass and laughed a little when I wiggled for him. He twisted it firmly into place. It felt a lot bigger than it looked and I lifted my head up off Adam as Neal tapped it a few times. "Oh."

Neal slid up behind me and lifted me so that I was kneeling on my knees. Carefully, he maneuvered me astride Adam's lap. He dropped an unopened condom on Adam's stomach and then nuzzled against the side of my neck. "Ready for more?"

"Yes." I bit down on my lip as his big hands drifted up from my hips and then cupped both of my breasts. I was very ready for more.

Adam watched us as he rolled on the condom, his eyes dark with arousal, a small smile playing on his mouth. They lifted and shifted me into place, both moving confidently and without a care in the world. I'd never felt safer in my life as Neal lowered me onto Adam's cock. Was it supposed to be like this? I couldn't really keep them both in my life, could I? Did I want to spend the rest of my life as a woman two men shared? Could we keep it a secret long-term? Would they eventually become jealous of one another? Would their friendship suffer if I was always between the two of them?

Neal bit down on my shoulder as I arched against Adam's penetration and I was lost. The pleasure of being full and the hot pain of his teeth overwhelmed me. When he started to rock us both into a hard rhythm I could do nothing but go along. His fingers clenched on my nipples, his chest dampened against my back and Adam shifted and thrust up against me with each downward plunge.

Gluttony is a sin. A delicious sin when applied to such a thing as pleasure. Adam arched underneath me and his eyelids literally fluttered closed as he came, his big strong body bowed and tight beneath mine. I rubbed one hand down the center of his chest and groaned just a little when Neal pulled me off Adam's cock.

Neal rolled me onto my back on the mattress, hooked both of my legs over his shoulders, and slid his cock right into me. The sting of new penetration took my breath away and each thrust of his body seemed to rock the butt plug that was still snug in my body. I felt like I was being used but wasn't remotely ashamed by that. Neal's hands tightened on my hips as he powered into me and then Adam rolled onto his side to watch us.

I was so ready to come again that I couldn't even speak. As if they understood that, Neal slowed his stroke inside me and tightened his grip on my hips. "Rub her clit for me, Adam. Hard, tight little circles."

Adam snaked his hand down across my stomach and right between my legs without a single hesitation. His fingers caught in what little pubic hair I allowed myself and played with the damp curls briefly. Then he slid two between my swollen labia and did as instructed. Soon, his strokes were matching Neal's beat for beat. It was not enough and too much all at the same time. I didn't know how I was supposed to survive something so good and so torturous.

The pressure increased and then, suddenly, it was there. The orgasm was so fucking amazing that I could barely even think. I screamed and went limp. Neal lowered me gently to the mattress and then pushed into me hard three times. His body went rigid and a low groan escaped his lips as he came.

I woke, still naked and snug between two male bodies. The butt plug was still very much in place and I had large, warm hands roaming over my body in a way that was both soothing and arousing. Adam nuzzled against my throat and then lifted his head to brush his lips over mine. I'd always known he would be one of those people who was easy with physical affection.

"You okay?" Neal asked, his voice warm against the back of my neck.

"Yeah." I stretched under their hands and sighed. "How long did I sleep?"

"Just about thirty minutes." Adam brushed my hair from my forehead and looked intently into my eyes. "Sleep or more?"

"More." I laughed softly when he grinned at my response. I felt greedy and overpleasured already. I could hardly wait for more.

"You are perfect," Neal murmured as he slid one hand down and adjusted the plug. He chuckled when I pressed back against his hand. "What about work tomorrow?"

"I'm off until Monday. What with my interview and all." I sighed and rolled onto my back between them. "Maybe I should cancel that."

"Afraid of it?" Neal asked.

"No, I just . . . I've never really wanted to be on television. I have no desire whatsoever to be famous, not even for a few minutes on a local station. I sort of hate Jean Turst."

"Well, I think you're entitled to be a little pissed at her," Adam admitted. "She hasn't made life easy for any of you. What do you think Tara's father will do?"

"Buy the newspaper she works for and make her life hell. That's what he does. I mean, he won't be evil or do anything illegal but she'll be regulated to writing articles about poodles and fashion week unless she quits. It's a little hinky for me because I don't really approve of censorship but she's such an asshole."

"Who tried to blackmail you." Neal tapped my nose. "Don't feel sorry for her. Andrew Marcus has never struck me as the kind of man to act amorally. He'll get to the bottom of things and make it go away quietly."

"I just hope it really is about money and not her nerd boyfriend." I rubbed the bridge of my nose and sighed. "My senior year I broke up with the guy I'd been with for years and

Jean's fiancé ended their engagement the same day and literally offered me the engagement ring he'd taken off her hand a few hours before. He said I was the love of his life."

"Not if he offered you a ring that he bought for her," Adam frowned as he said that. "You know, you hear about things like that but you just can't imagine anyone you know doing something so stupid."

"Oh, yeah?" I laughed. "What's the worst reason you ever broke up with a woman?"

Adam flushed and Neal started laughing. "Shut up."

Neal leaned down and kissed my mouth before rolling away and leaving the bed. I watched him walk into my bathroom, pleased with the play of muscles as he moved. After a few seconds, I turned to look at Adam, who'd obviously been watching Neal, too. At least we were both in the same appreciation society. I wondered if he realized how much his face gave away in that moment.

"Worst thing you ever did?"

Adam sighed and then bit down on his lip. "I broke up with a woman because her birthday was on the fifteenth."

"I don't . . ." I chuckled. "Her birthday was bad luck?"

"I wore the number fifteen for a month in college and in that time I broke two fingers, fouled out of four preseason games, and nearly lost my scholarship." Adam flopped back on his back. "So, I asked my coach for a new number."

"And your problems stopped?"

"Well, yes." Adam chuckled. "So, my first year in the pros, I'm dating this girl named Dana. I had a car accident on the way to our first date, a flat tire on our third, and got in a fist fight on our fifth. I broke my hand in the fight and was benched for the last two games of the season."

"Then he finds out her birthday is April fifteenth and dumps her by e-mail because he figures if he sees her again he'll get something like his leg broken." Neal finished as he came back into the bedroom with a towel and a few damp washcloths. He tossed one to Adam as soon as he reached the bed. "She calls me in tears and wants to know what she can do to change his mind."

Adam groaned. "Seriously, shut up."

Neal just laughed. "So, I told her that he was in a bad place emotionally and she was better off without him. I mean, he broke up with her in an e-mail."

I grinned and took the washcloth from Adam's hand. I eased him completely onto his back and slid astride him. He let me run the cloth over his chest, teasing at his nipples casually before I slid it down between us and cleaned his cock and then his balls. "I should tell you a secret, then."

"Yeah?" He asked, his voice a little hoarse. "I thought you'd already revealed your big secrets."

"You'd think." I wiggled on his lap. "I broke up with the last guy I dated through his secretary."

"You broke up with his secretary?"

"Yep, and the man before that . . . I broke up with his mother." I tossed the washcloth onto the floor beside the bed and sat back on his thighs. "At Sunday brunch at the country club where she'd invited me so we could have a talk about her baby boy and what would be expected of me if I married into her family. She made it sound like the Mafia."

"Did the guy protest this at all?"

"Never heard from him again, which proved to me that I'd made the right choice. He was obviously a mama's boy and the girlfriend wins that war. It's just not worth it."

Neal slid up behind me, also astride Adam's thighs, and ran a warm washcloth across my breasts gently. "You're right. A

217

mama's boy is a nightmare. Even the gay ones are unbearable. The last one I dated, I did my best to shock her so much that she would disown him or make him break up with me."

I leaned back against his chest as he teased my nipples erect and then pushed the cloth between my legs. "Did it work?"

"Hell, no. I had to dump him." Neal pressed against my shoulder as I laughed. "Do you know how much trouble it is to dump a gay man?"

"No clue." I sighed. "Well, there was this guy after college that I had to break up with because I figured out he was gay and he didn't know. That was difficult."

Adam shifted under us and ran his hands up my thighs. "Did you tell him?"

"Yeah, I did. He's been in a committed relationship with my brother for a few years. They're going to have a baby and a commitment ceremony."

Neal laughed against my neck. "That doesn't bother you?"

"No, he's a great guy." I relaxed against him as he cupped both of my breasts. The arousal building low in my stomach was softer than what I'd dealt with earlier in the evening but it was very nice. "I set him up with my brother for . . ." I laughed. "Well, I asked my brother to teach him how to meet guys and all that stuff so he wouldn't get hurt. Next thing I know they are living together in utter gay domestic bliss. They both get me presents on their anniversary every year."

Adam lifted his hips a little and I took his silent demand for what it was and took his cock in hand. He was hard and already leaking a little. I rubbed my thumb in the pre-cum gathered on the head and without even thinking about it lifted my hand and offered my wet thumb to Neal. Adam and I both shuddered when Neal sucked it into his mouth without hesitation.

"Christ, you'll be the death of me." Adam groaned as I

started to stroke him with my free hand. "He's right, you're perfect."

Neal released my thumb and laughed. "Yes, she is." He slid his hand down my stomach and cupped my pussy.

I couldn't help but look down to watch. His fingers delved between my labia and his knuckles brushed against Adam's balls with each stroke. One glance at Adam's face confirmed that this wasn't a problem. In fact, Adam tilted his hips and rocked against the stimulation.

"I think he's ready for more, too," Neal murmured against the back of my neck.

"Agreed."

"Are you going to give it to him?" Neal asked.

"I think we should both give it to him." I tilted my head and watched Adam flush with pleasure. "Isn't that what you want, Adam?"

His laugh was shaky and a little breathless. "You're an evil woman, Kris, pure evil. You can have anything you want."

"What about Neal?" I asked. "Can he have anything he wants as well?"

"Yes," Adam murmured with a groan. "Yes, God, just fuck me. I need . . ."

Neal moved away from us and returned with a condom for Adam. His hands slid around me and I watched as he tore open the package and then tossed the wrapper aside as I released Adam's cock. Everything stilled for a moment and then Adam gave a shaky nod. Neal pressed closer to me and started to roll the condom into place. Adam took a deep breath, his hips lifting against us in a way that felt almost helpless.

"He's never touched you like this before?" I asked softly.

"Not that I remember," Adam admitted. His cheeks were dark and his pupils were blown wide open.

"Do you like it?"

"Yeah."

Neal took a deep breath and pressed closer to me as he lifted his hands from Adam's cock. "So do I."

I lifted at Neal's urging and took a deep breath as they shifted so that I could lower myself onto Adam's cock. It was a replay of earlier but it occurred to me then that they'd been preparing me for this with that first time. Letting me get used to being pressed between them. I let my head fall back as I settled on Adam's cock to the hilt. I was going to sit funny for the foreseeable future but I was perfectly okay with that.

"Come here, baby, lay on me." Adam pulled me forward and cupped the back of my neck as I did as he instructed. "You ready for this?"

"Yeah." I pressed a kiss against his chest as he started to rub my back with one hand. His other clamped onto my hip to keep me still.

Since I was pinned in place I did my best to relax and lay on him. I closed my eyes at the click of the lube being opened and jerked only briefly when Neal grasped the plug and twisted it. He tugged a few times and then started to fuck me with it. Each thrust was controlled and exquisite. I groaned in disappointment when he finally pulled it free and they both chuckled at my lack of patience.

Neal pressed two lubed fingers into me and I jerked just a little. "Relax, sweetheart, I just need to make sure you're stretched enough. I don't want to hurt you."

"Okay." I closed my eyes and bit down on my lip as he added a third finger and started to thrust in and out of me. Adam shifted underneath me and I raised my head to look at his face. "What?"

"I can feel it," he admitted in a whisper. "Christ."

"Yeah?"

"Oh, yeah."

"You're going to feel his cock, too." I leaned down and nipped at one of his nipples. "Sliding against yours. I'll be tight and he'll be fucking me—fucking us both, really."

Adam shuddered. "Dirty. Christ, I never knew you'd be this dirty."

"Disappointed?" I asked, amused.

"No, I think we won at life when we found you." He shifted underneath us and Neal laughed a little.

"Okay," Neal murmured. "We're ready. I need you both to relax for me."

Adam's hand tightened on my hip and we both took a deep breath as Neal replaced his fingers with his cock. I arched up against the invasion, unable to help myself. Neal steadied me with one hand on my shoulder and pressed without pause into me until his groin was flush against my ass.

"Fuck." Adam groaned as he took a deep breath. "Somebody has got to move!"

I laughed, a little stunned, and Neal lowered his head to rest between my shoulder blades. It was delicious to be so full and I wiggled a little between them. They both groaned and Neal lifted his head.

"You stay still," he muttered and nipped my shoulder. "Let us do the work."

Neal pulled away and then started to thrust in and out with deep, sure movements. Each stroke sent a shiver down the length of my back. After a few strokes, Adam started to meet him, lifting his hips against us both. They held me tight between them, both of them fucking in and out of me with strength and power. I'd never wanted like this before; I'd never been wanted like this before.

I couldn't move, didn't think I'd ever want to move again. My vision darkened around the edges and I came. The orgasm was just there, rushing over me in a hot wave of pleasure that bordered on pain. "Fuck. Fuck." I braced both of my hands on Adam's chest. "Just . . . fuck."

"We got you," Neal promised. "And we're going to fuck you until you pass out."

"Yes, yes, please." I bit down on my lip and tasted blood. "Yes, fuck me."

Adam's fingers dug into my hips, his nails scoring my skin as he fought for purchase. "God . . . Kris."

"Can you feel him?" I asked, curling my fingers against his pecs. "Do you like it?"

"I love it," Adam admitted, breathless. "You're hot and wet and he's hard, pressing up against my cock."

Neal groaned against my neck. "Jesus."

"Come on," I whispered. "Fuck me, fuck us both."

Their hands tightened on me and I knew I'd find bruises in the morning but none of it mattered as they both began to thrust into me with hard, powerful strokes that left me jarred and moaning. Neal slid one hand down between my legs and pressed against my clit as he increased his pace. I was coming again in seconds. I screamed with it and would have collapsed between them if they hadn't been holding me in place. Adam thrust up against me and came with a low broken moan and Neal followed, his hips snapping against my ass four times before we all three collapsed on the bed.

Boneless, I couldn't even gather up enough energy to let Neal know he was crushing me, but obviously he knew since he pulled out of me carefully and rolled to lay on his back beside us. Adam pressed a kiss against my forehead and then pulled out of me and slid over so he could deposit my body onto the mattress between us. I just rolled onto my stomach and my forehead rubbed against the sheets. They both left the bed but I didn't bother to look. I figured they'd gone into the bathroom to clean up and just moaned a little when they returned with fresh washcloths.

I endured the cleanup with little protest and sighed when they pulled a sheet over me. "Thanks."

"Welcome, baby." Adam ran his fingers through my hair. "Should we stay or should we go?"

I lifted my head and frowned at him. "You want to leave?"

"Of course not, but this is going to have to be your call."

I looked at Neal, who was regarding me with dark, serious eyes. I realized then that I was making a pretty big decision. If I let them stay, they were going to try to stay forever. "Stay."

"Both of us?" Neal asked gently.

"Yeah, both of you." I waited until they'd both slid back onto the bed and under the sheet with me. "Best package deal I ever got."

Adam groaned and Neal laughed.

I snuggled between them. "And . . . Sonya is going to have a cow."

"Not Tara?" Neal asked, clearly amused.

"Nah, it isn't like she can talk . . . not with the kinds of games she likes to play." I grinned when they both started laughing. "Besides, life is too short not to get what you want."

"Agreed." Neal kissed my mouth. "We'll give you everything you want, Kris."

"I know." Maybe I'd known it all along.

Turn the page
for a preview of
Vonna Harper's "Mustang Man"
in TEMPTED BY A COWBOY!

On sale now!

1

Dust swirled around the legs of the two dozen mustangs trapped in the large corral. Beyond the wood enclosure waited the typical high desert offerings of dried grasses, hearty shrubs, low hills, and endless miles of wilderness. Occasionally, one or more of the wild horses stopped its uneasy movements and lifted its head to stare at the horizon.

From where he stood on the other side of the corral, cowboy and horse wrangler Miguel Perez easily read the mustangs' body language. Born free, they wanted nothing more than to return to the land of their birth. But it wasn't going to happen because they'd been on acreage that was the responsibility of the Bureau of Land Management. After due consideration, the bureau had declared that there was too much horseflesh for the acreage.

"I don't like it any more than you do," Miguel informed them, speaking from the depths of his heart. "Wild's all you've ever known. No matter what happens out there, you believe you should be allowed to live the way nature intended." Not taking his eyes off the thousands of pounds of hearty and well-fed horseflesh, he fell silent.

An ache ground through him, burning his eyes and making his fingers clench. Restless in a way that had been part of him since early childhood, he absorbed the mustangs' energy.

In his mind's eye, he slid between the wooden slats and approached the tall black stallion with the lightning-shaped blaze running down his face and flowing mane and tail. Seeing the human approach, the stallion would rear, his eyes showing too much white, nostrils flared. Standing his ground, Miguel waited for the animal to settle. Then he'd stepped forward and placed a calming hand on the stallion's muscled neck.

It's all right, all right. Everything's changed for you, but you'll survive. We're in this together, you and me. I understand you, and you'll come to understand me. To trust. To love. Maybe even to comprehend that I had no choice but to step into your life.

The grind and groan of an approaching vehicle pulled him back from his thoughts, but as a dust-caked BLM truck bounced into view, he left a small part of himself with the stallion he'd already named Blanco in honor of the white blaze. The journey toward their becoming one had begun.

After stopping some thirty feet away, the truck's driver silenced the engine. As the mustangs had done when Miguel had pulled in with his truck and single-horse trailer, they galloped to the far end of their enclosure. Both truck doors opened. Miguel took quick note of the driver, a tall, robust man in a standard brown BLM uniform who appeared to be in his early forties. His thinning hair was close-cropped and his boots, although dirty, were sturdy looking. Then he turned his attention to the passenger.

He hadn't expected to see a woman out in the middle of nowhere, especially not one about five and a half feet tall with slender arms and legs and a double handful of long, dark hair that she'd caught at the nape of her neck with something he couldn't see. Her close-fitting uniform revealed never-ending curves. His first reaction was that BLM needed to hire sturdier women for the physically demanding work.

His second spawned from his cock. He couldn't remember the last time he'd had sex, several months for the simple reason that managing ten thousand plus beef cattle on a massive and remote ranch didn't lend itself to frequent interactions with the opposite sex.

As the two closed in on him, he read her name tag: DAWN GLASS. She looked like a dawn all right, with lively hazel eyes that swept over her surroundings and then settled on him. Appraised him. Everything about her expression said she loved and embraced life. She was either deeply tanned or, like him, came by her dark coloring naturally. But whatever her nationality, she wasn't Hispanic. He would have known.

"You must be Miguel Perez," the man whose name tag identified him as Brod Swartzberg said. "From what you said, we figured you'd be the first to get here."

Miguel had called the number he'd been given via cell a couple of hours earlier to make sure he had the location right. At the time he'd spoken to a man, probably Brod, which had added to his assumption that he'd be working solely with men. From the way Dawn studied her coworker, he concluded Brod outranked her. As for why she'd chosen a career devoted to managing public lands mostly in the middle of nowhere instead of availing herself of civilization's comforts . . .

"How many others are you expecting?" he asked, directing his question at Dawn.

"Today, three," she said, still meeting his frank gaze. "A couple more tomorrow and what, five or six next week. We were hoping for a greater response to the program, but it's a large investment in time and effort."

Miguel knew that she was talking about the program in which qualified horse trainers had been invited to compete to see who could do the most with a wild mustang within a set time frame. Although the wranglers would be financially reimbursed to a certain extent, she was right, only a fool would get into the competition for the money.

Money had nothing to do with his reasons for having come here. Doing what he could to ensure a future for at least one of the mustangs drove him.

"How long have you been here?" Brod asked. "Long enough to get a feel for the animals?"

A "feel" for horses, as the other man called it, came as naturally to him as breathing. It was human beings he wasn't sure he'd ever figure out, not that it mattered. "I'm interested in the black stallion, the one with the white blaze."

Dawn and Brod exchanged a look. "Are you sure?" she asked. Once more her gaze leveled on him, and her eyes darkened, letting him know she was trying to dig beneath his surface. "This herd's been here nearly a month, long enough for them to get used to hay and for us to study them and ensure their health. He's the resident stud, probably sire to the majority of foals."

"That's what I figured."

She didn't understand his decision, or more likely, she didn't understand him. But she wanted to. Otherwise, she would have dropped her gaze, right? Wouldn't have sent a sensual zinging his direction.

Dawn Glass wasn't a beautiful woman, not in the way of the creatures who wound up on magazine covers. Her hands, although small like the rest of her, sported a number of tiny scrapes and scars. They were strong looking in keeping with her muscled forearms and what he could see of her thighs and calves. He didn't think she was wearing makeup and was close enough that he'd be able to smell her perfume if she was wearing any.

A woman who didn't think of herself as one, or so deeply female that the exterior package didn't matter? There'd been a zing, right? It hadn't all been his imagination, or had it?

What was he thinking? Hadn't he just allowed as how he didn't *get* humans? His interest in what made her tick was a by-product of having gone too long without sex and standing nearly toe to toe with a ripe example of the other half of the human race. Her breasts, although his fingers itched to explore them, didn't appear to be overly large, and her pants didn't tightly cup her crotch. She wasn't giving him a come-hither look or planting her hands on her hips, no moistening of her lips. Still . . .

Damn it, he was here to pick up a mustang to take back to the spread west of Yreka where he'd given the last three years of his life. No way would she let him throw her into the trailer and haul her there with him.

"You're experienced?" Brod asked. "Of course you are or you wouldn't be here. Even before I was assigned to the mustang project, I was curious about what it takes to change a bronc into a child's saddle pony. More guts than I have."

Shrugging, Miguel turned his attention back to the corral. As had happened when he'd first seen the wild horses, his heartbeat kicked up. In his mind's eye, he saw his beautiful and equally wild mother sitting high and proud and fearless on a bare back. Galloping full-out, she lifted her head and laughed as the wind threw her hair in an ebony stream behind her.

Untamed. A creature of the land.

Like him.

"You're committed to the natural horsemanship's gentling techniques?" Dawn asked. "I know you had to sign the contract saying you'll adhere to every aspect of the approach, but if you have the slightest hesitation about what you're being required to do—"

"Hold up, Dawn," Brod interrupted. "There's no reason for us to get off on the wrong foot with, what did you say your name was? Sorry but the trainers are all running together in my mind."

Extending a hand in the man's direction, Miguel introduced himself. After shaking Brod's hand, he turned toward Dawn. For just a moment she stood with her arms by her sides and her head tilted to the side. Then she placed small but strong fingers in his paw. A current of heat raced through his heart and headed south. Even when they broke off the contact, she kept her gaze on him.

Heat, everywhere. A wildfire waiting for the wind to turn it into a monster.

What was she looking for, maybe trying to reconcile herself to his Hispanic heritage? Maybe trying to make sure he wasn't lying about his commitment to natural horsemanship? If she went back with him, she'd soon understand how foreign the concept of breaking a horse's will and spirit was to him.

"You didn't answer me," she said. "You're completely onboard with the program?"

"Why don't you watch and find out."

Damn but Miguel Perez had a scrape-the-nerve-endings voice, Dawn acknowledged. The wind's love affair with his ink-black, nearly shoulder-length hair wasn't helping her maintain her equilibrium and she wasn't about to acknowledge the effect his molded-to-his-hard-ass-jeans was having on her libido. If their handshake had gone on any longer, she'd have been forced to press her thighs together.

Turning her face into the hot breeze did nothing to cool her cheeks. She could only hope her tan hid her flush. From the moment she'd spotted Miguel standing alone and self-contained near the corral, her day had spun in a full circle. Yes, she was accustomed to living and working in a male-dominated world. Yes, she'd been the recipient of more than her share of come-ons and responded to a handful of them. But seldom did she feel as if she'd been sucker punched.

Turned on and hot to fuck.

Primitive to primitive, no boundaries established and no quarters given. Going at it, just the hell going at it.

Teeth clenched in defense against the primitive bitch who'd suddenly made an appearance between her ears and thighs, she worked at making sure her eyes weren't bugging out of their sockets.

Male. Five hundred percent male. Dark and strong, right at six feet with a sinfully flat belly. Shoulders broad enough to hold their own against any and all bucking broncs, eyes straight out of midnight, a simple blue T-shirt too damn in love with that solid chest and washboard abs. And the jeans, the damnable jeans. And a cowboy's thighs and calves beneath the denim.

"The stallion you're interested in," Brod said, sounding a thousand miles away, "is on the upper end of the age we prefer to work with. The vet tried to look at his teeth to get a more exact age, but he wasn't having any of that."

After a quirk of his mouth she felt in her belly, Miguel started toward the corral. Against everything that made any kind of sense, she studied his stride or rather what walking did to his buttocks. Only belatedly did she think to catch up with her supervisor who was following Miguel. By the time she reached the two men, Miguel was lifting a leg in preparation for climbing over a rail and entering the corral.

"What are you doing?" she blurted, her four years with BLM and the last four months devoted to the mustang project kicking in. "Are you crazy?"

He swiveled toward her, leg hooked over a rail and hands on

the one above it. The sun settled on his features, giving them depth and stealing her breath. "Getting to know my horse," he said.

"On foot, without a rope, alone?"

He answered her concerns without saying a word. *I know what I'm doing,* his eyes said. *And I don't need or want you questioning me.*

But if he got hurt, if he wound up with broken bones and a bleeding body . . .

Remember what I said, his eyes responded. *I don't need you. Or anyone.*